THE BOSS

To Serve and Be Served

mischief

Mischief
An imprint of HarperCollins*Publishers*
77–85 Fulham Palace Road,
Hammersmith, London W6 8JB

www.mischiefbooks.com

A Paperback Original 2013

First published in Great Britain in ebook format by
HarperCollins*Publishers* 2012

A catalogue record for this book is
available from the British Library

ISBN-13: 9780007553211

Find out more about HarperCollins and the environment at
www.harpercollins.co.uk/green

Contents

CONTENTS

Never Enough
Kate Pearce

'So, this is where the big boss hangs out when he comes over here?' Josh hissed in Meredith's ear. 'It's pretty awesome, if you ask me.'

Privately Meredith agreed with Josh, but she wasn't going to gush. She'd leave that to her more exuberant friend.

Will, her other companion, studied the airy, open outdoor deck more carefully. 'I love a house on the beach and this one is sick. Do you think he owns it, or rents it?'

'Mr Clevedon of Clevedon Technology is *fabulously* rich. I say he owns it,' Josh declared loudly.

'I wish.' A soft laugh drew Meredith's attention away from the beach to where their host had come up behind them. A pleasurable shiver of anticipation crept over her. The man was fine and smart as hell. 'I *am* looking for a house, but the owners won't sell this one.'

Luckily, nothing ever fazed Josh who stuck out his hand. 'Thanks for inviting us to the company barbecue, sir. We lowly minions sure appreciate it.'

Robert Clevedon smiled to reveal white teeth and a dimple. Meredith guessed he was about fifteen years older than her, but he was still very, *very* fine. 'My secretary took care of all that, but I'm glad you came.' His interested gaze swept the three of them. 'I hear you were friends before you came to work for my company.'

'That's right,' Meredith said and made herself look him in the eye. 'We've been buddies since high school, and roomies too.'

'You share with two guys?'

'Sure. There are some drawbacks, but also some great advantages.'

He reached for her hand. 'Let me get you a drink and you can tell me all about it.'

Meredith let Robert lead her back into the house, aware of both Josh's delight and Will's mild concern. She accepted the margarita Robert made for her and waited while he topped up his own glass.

'Would you mind if I asked you a personal question, Meredith?'

She shrugged. 'It depends.'

'Well, I've been here at the West Coast office for a couple of weeks now, and I have to say I noticed you right away.'

'Because of my stunning beauty?'

He laughed. 'That, and the fact that you are very good at your job.'

Meredith felt her cheeks heat. 'Thanks. Are you going to promote me?'

'Yes, but that's a separate issue.'

She opened her eyes wide at him. 'You mean you're not offering me the opportunity to sleep my way to the top?'

His smile deepened. 'You have the brains to do it all by yourself.' He hesitated. 'And I assumed you had a boyfriend – if not two.'

'So?'

He moved a fraction closer, and she was aware of how tall he was and how he blocked her view of the party. 'I saw you in the parking lot kissing Josh.'

'I like kissing Josh.'

'And then I saw you with Will.'

'I like kissing Will too.' She met his gaze. 'I told you there were benefits in sharing a flat with two guys.' She waited for him to make some excuse and run away.

'Interesting.' He brushed his thumb over her lower lip and then glanced over his shoulder. 'Your guys are coming to rescue you. Don't forget to have a look around the house. The view from the master suite is phenomenal.'

Meredith nodded, and he left her with another charming smile to join his other guests. Josh and Will immediately claimed her and drew her towards the stairs away from the thump of the music.

'What happened?' Josh hissed. 'Did he hit on you? Will thought he was going to. I wasn't so sure.'

'I'm not sure either,' Meredith muttered.

'It's hard to tell with those Brits, isn't it? They are so … subtle sometimes.'

'He's Scottish.' Meredith finished the rest of her margarita in one cold frosty gulp. 'He said we could look around the house if we wanted to.'

Will took her hand. 'I'd like to. It's getting a bit crowded and loud in here.'

He started up the stairs, and Meredith and Josh followed him. To her surprise, the house had two more floors, opening up into a master suite that took up the whole of the top floor. Windows ran along the length of the back wall, giving a perfect view of the sun setting over the Pacific Ocean.

'Oh, it's beautiful,' sighed Meredith. She placed her hands on the glass and stared out over the pebbled beach.

Josh came up behind her and wrapped his arms around her waist. She shivered when he buried his face in the crook of her neck.

'You're trembling. Did that guy turn you on?' He slowly inhaled. 'She smells like sex, Will.' His hand slid down from her waist and under her skirt. 'Are your panties wet for Mr Clevedon?' His finger slid under her lace thong. 'Yeah, they are. Soaking wet.'

Will sank down to his knees and flipped up the front of her skirt. If anyone chose to take a stroll on the beach, they'd get an eyeful. Not that Meredith minded. Will licked the soft cotton of her panties, his tongue nudging and shaping her clit until she moaned.

'You want some of this, Meredith?' Josh bit down on her neck. 'Some finger-fucking and licking right here in Mr Clevedon's bedroom?'

'Yes,' Meredith breathed. They both knew what she liked, how turned on she got when they did this to her in public, how turned on they got.

Josh slid one hand under the halter neck of her dress. 'Leave her panties on for now, Will, let's make her beg.'

Will muttered something against her sex, his teeth teasing the lace edge of her panties while his tongue made the fabric even wetter, pushing it up inside her, making her want. Simultaneously, Josh pinched her nipple and Will thrust two fingers deep, making her gasp and arch against him.

'Yeah, that's it, honey. Take it.'

Behind them, the door opened. Meredith went still until she saw Robert Clevedon reflected in the glass. He locked the door behind him and came towards them, one hand in his pocket, the other holding a glass of wine. The sun glinted off the dark-auburn highlights in his hair. He took a seat and looked at Meredith. 'You don't mind if I watch, do you?'

'Meredith?' Josh asked. Will waited on her response too.

A wave of excitement flooded through her. 'I don't mind at all.'

It took her less than a minute to come, and less than three minutes more for her to come again. She found herself writing on the floor, Will's cock in her mouth and Josh's filling her cunt. They must have changed positions because when she finally opened her eyes it was to find Will slumped over her and Josh on his back on the carpet still gasping.

Her gaze flicked to Robert who wasstill watching them and sipping his wine. The only difference she could see was the thick evidence of his cock pushing against his jeans. He stood up and came across to them, his sharp blue gaze taking everything in.

'Meredith, will you stay with me, while the guys go and shower in the guest suite?'

Again, Will and Josh checked with her to see if she was OK, but she nodded and waved for them to leave. They wouldn't go far. And, if she were away for too long, they'd do anything to find her.

She put her hands flat on the floor and attempted to push herself up.

'No, don't get up.'

To her surprise, Robert put down his wineglass and joined her on the rug. He bent his head and kissed her already swollen mouth.

'I should probably shower.' She tried to move away, but he gently held her down.

'Why? I like you tasting like this.'

'Of other men?'

'Yes.' He kissed her again, his tongue in her mouth already experiencing both Josh and Will. 'I like you being well fucked but ready for more.' He paused. 'You are ready for more, aren't you?'

She sighed as he slowly lowered the zipper of his jeans and released his nice thick cock. 'Yeah. I always want more.'

'Even after two of them?'

'Yeah.'

'Me too. I could fuck all day.' He grasped his shaft around the base and rubbed the crown against her already swollen clit before sliding on a condom. She moaned as he thrust deep and held still.

'I want to fuck you without a condom like they did. I want you all wet from me.' He circled his hips and Meredith clutched at his shoulders. 'I'm totally clean and tested. You?'

'Me too.' Meredith whispered, echoing his earlier comment. 'I want you like that.' She swallowed hard. 'I've always liked being wet from a man, the smell of him on me, the way his come stays inside me.'

'Damn,' Robert groaned and moved hard and fast, each stroke shoving his full length into her until they came together. Without a word, he picked her up, placed her on the bed and stripped off what remained of her clothes and his own. Hiscock was already recovering, and she reached out to touch it.

He let her stroke him for a while, and then flipped her over onto her stomach and entered her from behind, his fingers seeking out her hard nipples and her equally hard clit, making her moan with each thrust. The smell of the condom mingled with the scent of sex. Meredith inhaled it all and loved it.

After he finally pumped himself deep inside her, he pulled out and rolled onto his back, settling her over him like a blanket.

'Do you want more of me, of this?'

'What do you mean?'

He kissed her throat. 'I'd like to fuck you a lot. I need to fuck you a lot.'

'But what about Josh and Will? Would you want me to stop having sex with them?'

'Not at all.' He came up on one elbow to look down at her. His auburn hair was rumpled, and the smile lines around his eyes much in evidence. 'Why would you think that?'

'Because most men don't like to share.'

'I like to share, and I like to watch. And, as I'm not going to be here all the time, I couldn't bear to think you were not getting fucked enough.' He cupped her chin. 'But, when I am here, I'd probably want you all to myself for at least a couple of days. Would you like that?'

Her breath caught as he nipped at her lip. 'I'd like.' She studied his aroused face. 'Girls aren't supposed to want sex all the time. If they do, they get the slut label.'

He moved her foot until it was balanced on his hip and slid back inside her, again without a condom. 'I want you to want it as much as I do.' He rocked his hips and she bit her lip. 'Are you sore?'

'A little.'She wondered if he'd pull out, but he didn't.

'I want to see you walk out of that door, and know that you're dripping wet because of me.'

She climaxed around his barely moving cock and his blue eyes narrowed. His fingers slid around to her clit. 'I want you to get wet every time you see me.'

'Just when you want it?'

He grinned. 'No, you can fuck me anytime you like.'

His fingernail grazed her clit and she came apart for him, the ache mingling with the pleasure into something new, something so different and dark she suspected she would learn to crave it. He reared over her and slowly started to come, each long pulse separate, filling her with his liquid heat. When he pulled out, he touched her between her legs, and then fed her his come from his fingers, adding his particular taste to Will's and Josh's.

'You'll stay the night.'

'Is that an order?'

'What do you think?' His blue gaze was as beguiling as his soft voice. 'I'm not going to keep you here against your will, but if you stay I'll expect you to do what I tell you.'

Her heart bumped crazily against her ribs. 'I'm not used to being told what to do.'

'I noticed that.' He cupped her breast and used his finger and thumb to pinch her nipple. 'You've got those two guys wrapped around your little finger. I'm not like that. I'll take everything I can from you, and then I'll take more.'

She couldn't look away from the calm certainty of his gaze. Could he really do that? Take her to a place she'd always craved but never found?

She took a quick unsteady breath. 'I'll stay.'

He bent to kiss her mouth. 'Good. Now get dressed and come back down to the party.'

She shifted on the already damp sheets and let her hand drift down between her legs. 'I still haven't showered.'

He got off the bed and stepped into his jeans. He picked up her cotton panties and put them in his pocket. 'You can shower later while I fuck you. I want you wet.'

'You want a lot, don't you?'

He smiled as he buttoned his blue shirt. 'I told you, I want everything.'

She slowly got dressed, washed as well as she could, and followed him down, where she found Will and

Josh on the dancefloor doing their own version of the Macarena. Robert was standing by the bar smiling down at some beautiful woman who clutched his arm. Meredith faced the other way and waved at her roomies. They waved back, but seemed determined to finish their dance.

She strolled across to the open window and studied the hazy coastline. She almost jumped when Robert came up behind her and handed her a fresh margarita.

'It's beautiful here. Quite different from Scotland.'

'I would think so. It's cold there, isn't it?'

He shrugged, the motion bringing his large body into contact with hers. 'Cold enough. Put your drink down and tell me what's along the coast from here.'

Meredith balanced her glass on the windowsill and pointed to the right. 'Keep walking this way and you'll end up in San Francisco.'

'Funny.' She shivered as his hand skimmed under her short skirt and cupped her mound. 'Tell me more. God, you're nice and wet.'

Unsteadily she pointed to the left. 'It gets better.' His fingers, cold from carrying the icy drinks, searched out her already swollen pussy lips and tugged on them. 'If you keep going that way, you'll end up in Los Angeles.'

'Really,' he murmured into her ear before biting down on it. 'You're better than my navigation system.' One long finger slid inside her and another circled her clit. 'Have you ever been clamped down here?'

11

'Clamped as in parking?' His answering chuckle tickled her skin. 'Oh, you mean that kind of clamp, sure.'

'Did you like it?'

'Yes.'

'Good to know.'

His fingernail grazed her clit and she bucked against his hand. He immediately moved closer, pinning her against the window frame. She wondered how many of the guests, the people she worked with, for God's sake, were looking their way, what they thought, what they could see ... Her cunt clenched around his finger and he stopped moving.

'Not yet, you haven't finished giving me my geography lesson.'

Meredith drew a very shaky breath and pointed straight out to sea. 'If you keep going for a few thousand miles that way, you'll get to Hawaii.'

'That's right.' He pinched her clit and she came hard, her hands clenched on the window frame. 'That's nice.' She sighed as he removed his fingers and brushed them across his mouth. 'Now, please finish your drink.'

He wandered away again but she didn't turn around. She wanted to follow him and see whether he'd openly caress her in front of the other guests. She'd probably let him; let everyone in her office see that what they'd always gossiped about was true. She was a slut and proud of it. The sun was disappearing fast now, an orange and red ball streaking the skyline into a crazy patchwork of tropical colours and long shadows.

Will and Josh came and stood on either side of her.

'Was he finger-fucking you just then?' Will asked quietly.

Meredith shuddered. 'Was it that obvious?'

'Only to us because we know how you look.'

'He asked me to stay the night.'

Will took her hand. 'And what did you say?'

'I said yes.' Meredith swallowed hard. 'He doesn't mind about you two.'

'That's big of him,' Josh grumbled. 'Mind you, I bet he is big.'

Will squeezed her fingers. 'You do what you want, roomie. And, if you need to come home in a hurry, just call us, OK?'

'Thanks, guys.'

Josh kissed her cheek. 'You're welcome, just as long as you share all the juicy details with us later.'

Robert joined them and smiled at Meredith over Will's head. 'Everything all right?'

'Sure. I was just telling Josh and Will that I plan on staying over.'

'Good.' Robert nodded. 'Do any of you need another drink?'

Meredith shook her head. Was it really as easy as that? No one was going to fight over her? Not that she wanted that, of course. Being civilised was so much better.

'I'm just going to the bathroom.'

Meredith retraced her steps across the dancefloor and passed the kitchen at the front of the house. The powder room was quiet and cool and gave her a moment to gather herself. When she unlocked the door, Robert stepped in, locked the door behind him and crowded her back against the sink. He kissed her hard and lifted her up until she sat on the marble countertop, then pushed up her skirt to expose her naked sex.

'Mmm …' He bent his head and held her open with his thumbs, licking and nipping at her pussy lips before thrusting his tongue deep inside her. She squirmed to get closer, blatantly rubbing herself over his working mouth and unshaven chin until she climaxed. He groaned his approval against her clit and one of his fingers slid back to rim her asshole before venturing inside. She braced her hands on the cold marble as he pulled away, his face wet with her juices, his eyes narrowed and so blue that she felt as if she was looking at the ocean again.

'Take out my cock and suck it.'

He slid a hand around the back of her neck, bending her forwards until she could unzip his jeans and release his hard hot length. She licked him like an ice cream, and he pushed against her lips until she took him deep, swallowed him down and sucked him in a regular driving pattern. He groaned her name, brought a hand round to her ass and flipped up her skirt. She smelled the rose soap by the sink and then his slick finger sank into her ass and then another one. His thumb delved into her cunt.

'Have you ever had three guys, Meredith?' he murmured. 'Fucking you, filling you?'

She couldn't answer him with his shaft stretching her throat, but she came for him, let him know how much his words excited her.

'Fuck, I'd like to be part of that. Three of us on you until we ran out of come.'

He grunted and shoved his hips forwards and came down her throat, holding her head so that she had to take everything. Not that she wanted to move, not that she wanted to be anywhere but where she was right now with him all around her. She waited until he relaxed his grip on her hair before sitting upright again. He kissed her mouth, one hand still buried between her legs, the other pinching her nipples. She'd never felt so alive, so well used, so drunk on the smell and power of sex.

'We're not finished yet,' he whispered. 'I'm going to take everything from you tonight, strip you down to basics, make you think of nothing else but me and my cock and what I'm going to do to you next.' He nipped her breast through her dress, making her shudder. 'Maybe I'll fuck you in front of everyone. Get Josh and Will to help. Make you kneel at our feet and suck cock all night. I wonder if you'd be able to stop me?'

She finally found her voice. 'What if I didn't want to stop you?'

He moved back, slowly buttoned his jeans and washed his hands. 'Then we might have a problem.'

He unlocked the door and left. Meredith reached forwards and relocked it with fingers that shook. She was going crazy. Was she really contemplating publicly fucking the owner of the company and her two best friends at the company party? What about her colleagues? What about her hard-earned respect? She retied her halter neck and smoothed down her rumpled skirt. But the thought of making Robert Clevedon lose control was almost worth the risk.

The sun had disappeared below the horizon and a lot of the party guests had disappeared as well. The remainder were sitting watching something sporty on a big flat-screen TV. Meredith squeezed in on the end of the couch next to Josh and Will who scooted up to make room for her. No one bothered to put the main lights on, and the shadows lengthened throughout the room.

Meredith felt rather than saw Robert sit beside her. He leaned in close and murmured, 'I'm not much into American sports. I don't have a clue what's going on here.'

'I can help you with that,' Meredith whispered in return, allowing her hand to drop to his thigh and the bulge of his cock. Will glanced down at her and angled his shoulder to shield her and Robert from the rest of the party. When everyone started shouting at the umpire, she eased Robert's zip down and released his cock, wrapped her hand around him and worked him through her fingers.

He leaned against the couch, his arms spread along the back, and let her play with him. The soft wet sounds were easily covered by the noise of the TV. Unlike Will and Josh, he wasn't circumcised, and she enjoyed dragging down his foreskin to expose the tender flesh of his wet slit.

A roar went up from the TV viewers and Robert's arm came around Meredith's waist. In one rough motion, he lifted her onto his lap and down on his cock. She bit her lip as he filled her, then saw Will realise what Robert had done and nudge Josh. God, he was big and she was so over-sensitive now. One flick of his finger on her clit made her come and she had nowhere to hide, had to ride out the pleasure among the cheers for the local team.

Eventually Robert lifted her off him, his smile still firmly in place. He held out his hand and murmured just loudly enough for Josh and Will to hear him as well. 'I want all three of us to fuck you. I don't think we'll be missed for a while. Come upstairs.'

Meredith smiled at him and nudged Josh and Will until they also got up. She was finally going to get her perfect sexual fantasy. And even better, if she were lucky, every time Robert Clevedon was in town, that fantasy would become *her* permanent reality.

What the Maid Saw
Justine Elyot

They looked like an interesting couple. I watched them sidelong while I dusted a bust of some ancient lord or other, as they checked in at reception.

They had booked separate rooms, but were allotted the ones with the connecting door, whether by chance or prior arrangement I didn't know. Their dress suggested a working partnership, with him in the superior role. She was perhaps a PA or less senior member of the organisation. She let him do all the talking at the desk and hung back, fidgeting with her phone.

I admired her shapely bottom in its tight-fitting skirt and the curve of her calves, displayed to advantage by her strappy black heels. I imagined my hands on that arse, squeezing little dimples into the cheeks with my thumbs. I imagined those sky-high heels over my shoulders while I licked her sweet little pussy. Was he going to

18

do all that? Or were they genuine colleagues? Somehow, I didn't think so.

I was still in the lobby with my polish and dusters when they came down from their rooms for tea on the terrace. I applied a final wipe to a vase and hotfooted upstairs, keen to indulge my favourite hobby.

I am making a collection of photographs – call it an art project – of the guests' belongings. I think it will make an intriguing exhibition when it is finished. All the detritus of life is in it: the pill bottles, the discarded novels, the ripped stockings, the binned pregnancy tests, the dying anniversary flowers. Once, a gun. Another time, a crack pipe and a wad of money. But most of what I photograph is sexual. Vibrators, used underwear, handcuffs. He looks like a handcuffs man.

I opted for the room on the right, which appeared to be hers. It had all the typical feminine fixings. An evening dress hung on the outside of the wardrobe. Perfumes and lotions on the dresser. I opened the drawer, hoping for something shocking, but found only some electric chargers and a Gideon bible. Her underwear yielded no latex or leather, not even anything cheekily crotchless.

Perhaps I was wrong and they were simply a boss and a secretary spending a post-conference night here.

Footsteps on the landing threw me into panic. Had they changed their minds about the tea? I considered hiding in the wardrobe, but seconds later realised that they were both going into the room nextdoor.

His was the voice I heard first. 'I've told you about this before,' he said. 'You do not give orders. You leave the ordering to me.'

'But you were in the lobby, seeing about your newspaper. And they came to take the order. And I knew what you wanted.'

'None of that alters anything, Mara. You have broken a rule. And you know what happens when you break a rule, don't you?'

'Yes, Sir,' she said with a resigned sigh.

Mara might have known what happened when she broke a rule, but I didn't, and I very much wanted to. I tiptoed to the connecting door, knelt down and put my eye to the keyhole.

He stood by the bed with his arms folded while she – Mara – was rummaging in a dresser drawer. She had her back to me and, as she bent to retrieve whatever it was, her bottom was thrust out, tautening her skirt to maximum stretch. He was looking at it too, the dirty bastard, getting a good long eyeful.

She straightened up again, turned and handed him something. It was a leather strap, about half an inch thick, with a grip for the hand at one end.

I took a deep breath. I was in for a treat.

When he took the strap, he slapped it into his palm, as if testing its painfulness, then he nodded.

'You know what comes next,' he prompted, and the

lovely Mara dropped on her knees in front of him, head bowed.

'Please, Sir, I'm sorry I broke a rule and I beg to be punished for it.'

'I'm considering it.'

'Please, Sir. I really need it. Please punish me.'

'How hard?'

'As hard as you think I deserve.'

'Good.'

He was good. Very good. Making her beg for it – nice touch. I'd have to add it to my repertoire.

She bent to kiss his shiny shoes, her silky hair falling over her cheek. I pictured her bending like that to lick my clit, all so sweetly submissive and obedient. I raised my skirt to my waist and put my fingers down my knickers. Damn this stupid country-house hotel and its inconvenient uniform.

'We'll start with my hand,' he said, seating himself in the armless straight-backed chair by the bureau. 'Remove your skirt and place yourself over my knee.'

I watched her unzip, my mouth watering as I wondered which view of her I would have. Perhaps her face, suffering and contorting in pain. Or perhaps her bottom. I rather hoped for the latter.

Her tight skirt had been tugged down over the swell of her hips before I glimpsed her milky thighs, with their suspender straps interrupting the smooth expanse

21

of skin. She stepped out of it and laid herself gracefully over his lap. Joy of joys, I had the most perfect view of her upthrust bum, the flesh spilling from her silky shorts.

Not that the silky shorts lasted long, for he peeled them down until her bottom was bare and they rested just above her lace stocking tops. Now her arse was cunningly framed by the suspender belt and straps, with the froth of silk and lace three-quarters of the way down her thighs.

She was ready to begin. And so was I. My finger was on the button. Three, two, one …

But he wanted to lecture her first, it seemed, while his hand moved idly round and round her vulnerable cheeks. He spoke about mindfulness of rules, respect, discipline and duty. She chimed in only to say 'Yes, Sir' and 'No, Sir' but he seemed satisfied with this.

His palm flattened against her buttocks, which tensed immediately. I imagined her teeth and fists clenched in concert.

'Now this is just to start us off,' he warned her, starting in with quick, sharp smacks across the centre of her quivering bum. He did not seem to be putting a great deal of effort into it, lifting his arm only to chest height before swooping his hand down to meet her flesh, but the sound was music to my ears, as were Mara's wails and complaints.

'Oh! Ouch! Ouch! It hurts!'

'Don't be silly, Mara, this is a gentle warm-up. I haven't even started.'

A long, despairing moan met this statement, but I could see that the boss was warming to his work now, laying on harder and harder strokes, at times leaving handprints. It was strangely aesthetically pleasing to watch Mara's bum jiggling around and changing to a deep-pink colour under her employer's chastising hand and I watched transfixed, hoping that he would carry on for a very long time. Much as Mara disliked the slow, hard strokes, she seemed to hate the sudden volleys of speedy ones even more, for these made her wriggle and twist like fury, calling out for him to please, stop, please, it was too much, she would be good, oh, she would. But he was utterly resolute and no amount of gasping, pleading or tearful contrition would deflect him from his purpose. Only when Mara's poor bottom was fully and blazingly reddened and her kicking legs limp and spent did he begin to stay his hand.

For my part, my hand was hard at work, stuffed eagerly inside my cotton boyshorts, and I knelt with my fingers stroking the wiry curls of my muff and my longing clit, excited beyond expectation at Mara's humiliation.

Oh, why did it have to end? I silently protested. Mara's bottom had taken ten long minutes of this summary treatment, but I wanted to see more.

I uttered mute thanks to an unnamed deity when the

boss, helping his subdued secretary to her feet, instructed her to go and bend over the side of the bed with her bottom high and her feet apart. This was not the end!

My joy was not matched by Mara, whose lower lip stuck out a mile.

I wondered about this dynamic. Surely it must be consensual. They would have a safeword, presumably. He seemed highly experienced, at least, and they had clearly developed their own rituals.

'Mara, a spanking by my hand is the least you can expect for petty rulebreaking. Breaking one of the golden rules of obedience merits the application of something a little more forceful. If you are to learn, I must be strict and consistent with you. Do you understand?'

'I am too sore,' she snuffled.

'Do you understand, or shall I be harder on you than I originally intended? There will be extra strokes for defiance.'

Mara let out a great howl of anguish, but she went to the bed and obediently bent herself over the side, grasping the frame. Her sore bottom glowed like a beacon amid the pale-pink frilliness that framed it. I sucked in a breath on her behalf, then another when Mara parted her feet, as instructed. All at once, that gorgeous little slut's most secret and intimate parts were visible, tender pink lips spread and vulnerable. To me they looked edible and I imagined my teeth nipping and tongue licking at the tempting array.

But it seemed that Mara could not expect anything so pleasurable, as the boss had picked up that wicked-looking brown leather strap and stood testing it for bend and snappiness.

'Do you ever go anywhere without those nasty things?' blurted Mara, fearfully watching him stroke the supple hide then bend and flex it against his palm before slapping it gently down.

He looked over at her, strap in hand, without answering.

'You will count,' he said briskly, crossing to stand at her rear. 'I plan to apply twenty strokes, but I will give extra for broken position or disobedience of any kind. Now then.'

He swung the strap through the air a few times before allowing it to whistle down and snap across Mara's backside, causing her to sing out in pain and rock on her heels until she could count out a shaky 'One, Sir'.

I noted the wide red stripe left to burn across Mara's bottom and watched agog as the rest were delivered, slowly and with decorum, sometimes leaving a little pause for Mara to recollect herself, falling across the full width of her bum and down to the upper thighs, which appeared especially painful. I fidgeted furiously with my needful bud while I watched Mara lift her feet, clutch the bed frame and yelp into the mattress, as her bottom received stripe after stripe. The air around me smoked and snapped with the sounds and scents of punishment and arousal; the shocking crack of the strap urged my fingers on to the completion of the quest.

Mara earned herself two extra strokes by jumping up straight and rubbing her bottom furiously, and, by the time the twenty-second was applied and counted, I had found my moment of sweet release, biting my lip as she doubled over on the floor, intent on allowing no sound to betray me.

I shuffled back to my knees for a final glimpse of Mara's crimson bum with its pattern of long rectangles. The girl was panting and mewling, still bent over, while bossman was issuing some words of wisdom or other which went over my head, so transfixed was I by the obvious changes that had been wrought to Mara's cunt. Now it was deeper in colour, swollen and glistening slightly with what must surely be her female juices. It certainly seemed that Mara had taken some pleasure from the pain. It wasn't my bag – I used to think it was some myth made up to suit the purpose of cruelly inclined men. But I had seen enough juicy little pain sluts over the years, and here was Mara, almost dripping ...

I watched the errant secretary slowly uncurl her spine and stand, head bowed and bum burning, before her master.

He bent and whispered something into her ear. She grimaced and turned towards me and – oh, shit! – she was coming straight towards the door.

26

I didn't have time to stand straight, still less back away, before the handle turned. It was unlocked. I hadn't thought it would be unlocked. In my haste to scramble out of view, somewhere, anywhere, I fell backwards.

When the door opened, my fingers were still struggling to escape my knickers and my skirt was hiked around my waist.

Mara's hands flew to her mouth and she aimed a desperate look at her boss. So did I.

What the hell was going to happen now?

I retrieved my juice-stained fingers and tried to stand, blabbing out incoherent apologies. At least, they might have been apologies, or I might have just repeated 'Oh, God' over and over.

The boss, surprisingly unruffled, simply folded his arms and watched me. 'What have we here?' he said. Then he crooked a finger.

'Please don't report me,' I whispered, finally managing to arrange my legs and my skirt so as to allow me to get up.

He shook his head and shushed me.

I walked past the curious Mara and presented myself to the boss. I couldn't look at him, focusing instead on my fingers, which gripped each other so tightly they whitened around the knuckles.

'Who are you?'

'A chambermaid. Sir.'

'No, I mean what's your name?'

'Kim, Sir.'

'And what were you doing, crouched down there by the door?'

'I was ... polishing the handle, Sir.'

Even as I said the words, I knew lying was a bad idea, but I felt I had to make the token gesture, or he'd think I was some kind of pushover.

'Polishing the handle? Look at me.'

I twisted my neck to the side, but he repeated the instruction and I lifted my eyes with much reluctance to his.

'Do you often polish things with your hands down your knickers, Kim?'

I could do nothing but shrug.

'You were watching us, weren't you?'

'I couldn't help but notice ...'

'No, I'm sure,' he said dryly. 'And what did you notice?'

'You spanked her. Your secretary. And you used a belt. Strap. Thing.'

'That's right. So you saw everything, from start to finish?'

I nodded.

At this point, he looked away from me, towards Mara. 'I thought I sent you to fetch something, didn't I?'

Her mouth fell open and I thought she was going to protest, but she decided against it and headed into the other bedroom, her red bottom swaying from side to side.

28

'And what did you think of what you saw?' He spoke to me again, his voice lower this time.

'It was very interesting, Sir. I'm so sorry!' I burst out again.

'Don't apologise. Clearly, you found it quite stimulating. Didn't you?'

'Yes, Sir.'

'Did you come?'

I sucked in a quick breath. What a question.

'Yes,' I whispered.

'I see. So you like spanking?'

'Not really. It wasn't that, so much as ... watching her getting spanked. She's very pretty, Sir.'

'You like her?'

I nodded again.

'You're gay?'

'Yes.'

'Well, this is interesting.'

He was silent for a moment, his hand at his chin.

'Are you going to report me?'

'No. No, I don't think so.'

'Oh, thank you,' I blurted. 'Thank you so much. And I really am sorry ...'

'I haven't finished yet. Listen. You like Mara. How would you like to help me complete her punishment?'

I looked wildly back into the other bedroom. Mara was on the threshold, holding something in her hands. I couldn't quite make out what it was.

29

'Oh … is that … I mean, would that be OK?'

Her blushing face was bowed. She still wore a silky blouse on her top half, while her bottom half consisted only of stockings, suspenders and lowered knickers. Her little pink triangle was shaved bare, her pussy lips peeking out at me.

'Mara,' said the boss. 'Kim here would like to join us. I trust you will be a good girl for her. Won't you?'

'Yes, Sir,' she said.

'If she wants to,' I said, turning to the boss, suddenly firm. 'Only if she wants to.'

'She wants to,' he said.

'I need to hear it from her.'

'Fair enough. Mara?'

She raised her head and nodded shyly at me. Her blush was gorgeous. I wanted to kiss her lips and stroke her hair, especially when she gave me the tiniest little smile, a secret between us.

'Thank you, ma'am,' she said.

'Now,' said the boss, 'bring me the plug and then undress yourself, for Kim to watch.'

Mara handed over the item, which I saw was a butt plug, quite a wide model, not for beginners. Then she came to stand opposite me, so close I could touch her, but I wasn't sure it was allowed, so I held off.

She unbuttoned her shirt and slipped it off, then took off her bra to reveal beautiful full, plump breasts with round red nipples.

'Touch them, Kim,' invited the boss. 'Feel how heavy they are.'

They were rather heavy, not the weightiest I'd ever held, but certainly filling my palms satisfyingly. I let them jiggle in my hands, then I squeezed them, then I stroked the nipples with my thumbs and was rewarded with a pretty little shimmy of her hips.

'She has very sensitive nipples,' he remarked. 'The lightest of clamps is all she needs. But I'm not going to clamp them today. She's had her quota of pain. Feel how hot her bottom is.'

I slid my hand around her hip, on to the luscious curve of her arse. Oh, he was right. The heat was lovely, like warming my hands on a radiator. I loved the effect the strap had made, ridging her skin so I felt little ripples of sensation when I stroked it.

'Best of all,' said the boss, more softly now, 'is the effect a good thrashing has on her pussy. Touch it. You'll see.'

I looked up at her face, as if seeking permission, but her eyes were closed in a kind of rapture. She was somewhere deep inside herself but, wherever she was, it was exactly where she wanted to be.

I parted her thighs a little wider and dipped two fingers between her pussy lips. So hot and juicy, and her clit was swollen right up. I massaged it slowly, enjoying the way her thighs trembled against my hand.

'You're right,' I said to the boss. 'She's soaking wet.'

I pushed my fingers into her cunt, digging inside, feeling her tightness, while I kept my thumb on her clit.

'Hmm, careful there, Kim, you'll make her come. She's not to come yet.' He changed the subject brightly. 'Have you any experience with butt plugs?'

'A little,' I said. 'Not much.'

'But some? Oh, I'm sure you'll do a good job.'

He sat down on the edge of the bed and unbuttoned his trousers. 'Over here, Mara, on your knees.'

She knelt between his legs, waiting obediently while he removed his erect cock from his underpants.

'She's going to suck my cock while you put the plug in,' said the boss. 'Lubricant is in the right-hand drawer. Let me know when it's fully inserted.'

I blinked, a little nonplussed at the turn of events, but I retrieved the bottle of lube and went to sit on my heels behind Mara, who by now had a good mouthful of the boss's rather large cock.

I parted her buttocks, seeking the tiny round hole I had the task of filling. Her cheeks were hot and obviously still sore, and her little rosebud quivered when I pressed my thumb against it. She was obviously well trained, though, because she kept her bum thrust out and didn't try to clench or wriggle away from me.

I uncapped the lube and spread plenty on my fingertips, then I pushed them against the rosette, circling it delicately, getting closer and closer to the target. I felt a tiny pressure of resistance, then my forefinger eased inside. How tight she was. I thought she might suck my finger inside and hold it there, but I was able to pull it back with little trouble.

I applied a good squirt of lube to the plug and went to work on that next. I pushed it slowly and gently, rotating it until it began to slip in. As I pressed, then stopped, then pressed some more, she made scoffing noises, her mouth too stuffed to express her real reaction.

The boss was holding her by her hair, keeping her head low down. I wondered if she was deep-throating him. He looked pretty happy, at any event.

'How ... is it going?' he rasped.

'Nearly halfway in,' I reported. 'Just getting to that nice wide part.'

'Keep that held there for as long as you can before you push in the rest,' commanded the boss. 'Make her feel it. Make sure she really feels how full and stretched she is.'

'You're the boss,' I said. 'Now, keep still, Mara, and be a good girl. You're going to have a sore bum, but you won't mind, will you? Because it's what you deserve.'

I loved her little gasps of shock and amazement as I held the plug at the cruellest part. The boss shoved down hard on her head, fucking her mouth. She writhed at the hips and I took pity on her and pushed it all the way in, so that the flange sat between her cheeks, showing anyone who looked that her rear hole was occupied. How decadent it looked, with her striped scarlet bum cheeks on either side.

I wanted to touch myself again, but I knew better things were coming, so I held off.

'Good,' said the boss. 'Off, Mara.'

He let go of her hair and released her mouth from his thrusting cock.

'Now then, Kim, it's up to you what you want to do with your clothes, but you need to lie down on the bed with your legs spread and your cunt available for Mara to lick. I'll give you a moment …'

It barely took a moment. I threw myself eagerly on to the bed, pulled up my skirt, yanked off my knickers, layingmyself bare for Mara's tongue.

Soon enough it was there, planted between my lips, while she breathed and stroked and licked like an expert, kissing my clit and pushing her fingers inside my cunt with such absorption that you would never realise she was getting fucked from behind all the while. Her face lay buried in the junction of my legs, building my arousal higher and higher, while the boss, still almost fully clothed, rose behind her like a giant, his tie flapping this way and that, his cheeks growing redder, his veins beginning to stand out on his forehead.

I was the first to come, melting blissfully into that hot, eager mouth. She didn't withdraw her tongue, but kept on kissing my spread lips until she moaned into them, her own orgasm forced from her by the boss's purposeful thrusts.

He held on a while longer, seeming to enjoy his view enough to want to prolong it, but eventually he too joined us in our post-coital haze, collapsing on top of Mara's back with a roar.

'Well, Kim,' he said, once he had Mara over his lap to remove the plug. 'Thank you so much for your input, but I hope we haven't kept you from your duties.'

Oh. My duties. I should have finished polishing the silver in the drawing room ages ago.

'Oh, right,' I said, looking from him to her.

Mara smiled at me with lazy satiety. 'That was awesome,' she drawled. 'We'll come here again.'

'I hope you do,' I said, smoothing down my skirt. 'I really hope so.'

Without him, next time.

'Here's my card,' said the boss, handing it over.

It read: 'J Barraclough. Professional disciplinarian and dom. All submissive tastes catered for.'

'Oh! So you aren't …?'

'We have a purely business relationship,' said Mara. 'You can have my card too, if you want. Or just my mobile number.'

'I'd like that.'

Leaving the room with Mara's contact details, I praised whoever might be the patron saint of voyeurs. And, as I passed the bust of the old lord, I almost thought he winked at me.

Property Of
Sommer Marsden

'Winona,' he said. Just him saying my name sent a shiver up my spine. I turned a bit too fast and almost propelled myself out of my office chair. Which led to a nervous little titter.

Nice. Very sexy.

'Mr Bennett,' I said, nodding.

I wanted to look cool, but I felt like I was vibrating. How long would this last? I wondered.

He smiled as he put some papers neatly on top of his stack of folders. His suit was charcoal grey, his tie a navy blue, his shirt white. All very boring components that did nothing at all until you tied them all together by hanging them on a lean but muscular handsome man. A breath-stealing kind of handsome.

Trevor Bennett. My boss of all things.

'Can you come into my office, please?'

The word 'can' was a joke. He meant: 'Come into my office. Now.'

I nodded and cleared my throat. I had nothing to say, but he just made me feel that way. Like I had something stuck in my throat – maybe his cock. I bit my tongue to stop myself from laughing and then said softly, 'Coffee?'

'Already have some. We need to discuss tonight.'

Tonight? I had no idea, but I faked like I did and locked my computer. 'Coming,' I said.

That made him smile.

* * *

Trevor Bennett is a powerful man. He plays with money the way I used to play with dolls as a young girl. I followed him into his office, feeling like my legs were only a mirage. That they couldn't actually support me. My spiffy black slingback heels tip-tapped on the hardwood floor. They are his favourite shoes. I wear them often. And often when I wear them, they are all that I am wearing.

Trevor indicated a seat and I took it, smoothing my skirt primly because I knew it made him think dirty things. It often made him do dirty things shortly after thinking them.

'Tonight is the big wooing party. We bring in all the millionaires and billionaires and all those we want to bring into the fold. We woo them and wine them and dine them and try to convince them to let us play with their money.'

I nodded. Waiting.

'I'd like you to attend with me.'

I blinked and stared. Brilliant.

'I … um, I … of course.It's my duty as your assistant to –'

'As my date.'

Trevor leaned back against his desk and opened the button ofhis suit coat. I loved to watch him move that way – short, economical movements with no fluffery or wasted energy. He was a work of art. And he could make me come like I was dying. Brutal, wild, sweet – all the things orgasms were made to deliver.

'Your date?' I echoed. Flabbergasted. I had never in a million years dreamed it would ever go beyond fucking.

His smile said he knew that. Big grey eyes, as stormy as the weather in March, regarded me and my stomach tingled like I had swallowed a live electrical wire. My face was hot, my hands cold, my stomach and chest full of anxiety and, yes … excitement.

'Yes, as my date. I think we've gotten to that point, don't you?'

I could only nod dumbly. If I opened my mouth, something entirely mortifying would pop out, I was sure.

'You do know what they think of us? Don't you? You

and your pointy shoes or your big black boots? You and your fucking phenomenal ass and ice-blue eyes? And me in my big hot-shot office giving you dick-tation.'

I blushed and studied my lap. I bit my lip and tried to breathe. The toe of that pointy shoe was swinging like a metronome.

'Do you, Winona?'

I shook my head. 'No, Sir.'

'No, what?'

'No, Trevor,' I said.

The man was a paradox. Expecting – no, demanding – the exact opposite of what most dominant men demanded. He confused me and scared me and, oh, fuck, God, yes, he made me want him so badly all I could focus on was the thumping demand of my cunt.

'They think you have me pussy-whipped. But not just figuratively, literally. They think you are the one wielding the whip, as it were. And I am the one asking for one more, Mistress.' He winked and I shifted in my seat, trying to find a comfortable position for my poor, swollen, wanting nether bits.

'I had no idea.'

He straightened his trouser leg. 'Doesn't matter. I don't really give a shit what they think.'

'The mark of a true dominant.'

'But I find it amusing. I'd like to put a little trinket on you. So you remember when they all start flirting, and touching and joking ... that you are mine. Do you approve?'

Again, I nodded mutely. Maybe I had a future career as a ventriloquist's dummy.

'But, you know, some studded dog collar or bondage nonsense would look really stupid with a lovely cocktail dress and delicate sensual shoes. It would also be abysmal on that neck of yours.'

Thank God. The thought of something that tight to my throat made me jangle with fear and anxiety. I had a thing about my throat and he knew it. It was one thing to let him grip me there – his hand imprisoning my jumping pulse – while he fucked me. It was another to ask me to wear something constricting for hours and hours and not freak out.

'Thank you, Trevor.'

'So this was the thing I thought would help us celebrate our first date. Also celebrating the fact that you're mine now. You are mine now, aren't you, Winona?'

'Yes, Trevor,' I breathed. All of me felt like I was trembling. Inside and out. I pictured him eating me out, I pictured him fucking me with his fingers, I pictured him trussing me up and making me say his name until I wept it.

'Good girl. Property of Trevor Bennett. Come here.'

I went. I walked to him slowly until we were eye to eye and he kissed my hand once like a prince in a fairytale. 'There she is,' he murmured.

To Serve and Be Served

I stood like I was in the military. Back straight, legs locked, shaking like a motherfucker, but trying valiantly to hide it. He popped the big black velvet box and I waited, throat bared, as if for execution.

It was deceptive. Pretty and silver. Three jointed lengths of sterling silver with a Claddagh attached. The Irish symbol for friendship or love or marriage. It was gorgeous and bold and would go with anything at all.

But, when he held it up, my heart started to race. For, as pretty as it was, it was just as bad as the dog collar he'd dismissed. I could tell by its size that it would grip my throat with a cold clinical pressure that made me antsy. All I wanted to do was turn and run.

'Now I know how you feel about things on your neck,' he said. He ran his finger along my bottom lip and my body went haywire, distress and arousal mingling and making me feel floaty and spacey in my own body. 'But it's just until the party's over. To remind you. If you are a good girl, we'll take it off as soon as we can.'

I nodded and then bit my lip hard enough to taste a coppery kiss of blood. I would not cry. I would obey.

I bowed my head to allow Trevor to put the necklace on. Each section of sterling silver reminded me of a very subtle smiley face. The three were linked and the charm dangled from the centre section. I could tell just by eyeing it that it would be too snug to my flesh. Constricting and cruel.

41

That alone made my cunt wet. My heart beat fast. My cheeks flushed.

Trevor smiled and shook his head. He tsk-ed at me and I knew I'd made a mistake. 'Come on now, Winona … is that how you accept a gift?'

He pointed one blunt finger at the generic grey carpet at his feet. 'Kneel.'

I felt stupid. What had I been thinking? But again that wet curl of arousal in my pussy made it all OK. I moved forwards, dropped to my knees, bared my throat.

He hooked the necklace quickly. With my issues, it felt like a death sentence – the most severe of punishments. But I forced myself to take a shuddery but calming breath and relax some.

His zipper hissed at me and I watched, excited and some-what ashamed, to see him pull his cock free. He painted my lips slowly with the warm silken skin of his glans. I hummed softly, swaying a little on my knees as if intoxicated.

I parted my lips, let him smear his skin along my pink painted mouth. When he made that sound in the back of his throat that always made me tremble, I moved my head forwards to suck him.

'This is how you accept a gift, Winona.' His voice was soft as he pushed deeper into my throat. I swayed along with the lulling sound of his words. He took my head in his hands, cupping me so that the world was muffled and I felt like I could hear the ocean if I tried.

When he touched the back of my throat with his cock, driving deep, I gagged a little. My eyes watered. I sucked in a desperate elated breath through my nose.

He growled, a sound I cherished. 'Hike up that skirt, Winona. And there'd better be no panties under there.'

My fingers clutched my snug skirt and lifted. Beneath it I wore only thigh-high stockings and a small, well-groomed patch of pubic hair.

He nodded, forcing his cock deeper into my throat. 'Good' was all he said. And then, 'You may touch yourself.'

I was slick and slippery. Warm and eager. My fingers slid along my nether lips, parting, stroking, plucking, pinching. I eased fingers into my cunt as I sucked him a little faster. A little deeper. A little better.

His fingers dug into my loose chignon, pulling just enough to give me that welcome element of pain. All the while the necklace that he gave me kept its greedy metal fingers on my pulse, the swell of my throat, the charm banging the hollow at my clavicle. Mocking me.

He yanked my hair hard when he came and that bright burst of pain pushed me over the edge. I climaxed a second later, shivering fingers buried in my soaking wet pussy, my clit throbbing in time with my heart.

He took my hand and helped me stand after tucking himself back in. Always he treated me as if I were royalty. Some great beauty, some wonderful lady, to be admired and cherished. Until she was used and abused. Spanked and bound and whipped and fucked. Although I knew that was only him cherishing me all the more.

I wiped my lips with a tissue he handed over and then he kissed me. Almost a perfunctory kiss, but not quite. His tongue snaked out at the very last second, sneakily taking a taste of his semen on my lips. It always turned me on when he allowed himself to go there. He'd once whispered, 'One of these days, I'm going to clean up after myself when I come. And then I'll fuck you again. What do you think?'

I think I'm still waiting for that day because I might actually die of arousal.

'I think tonight will be interesting. Fun. Wear that red wrap dress with the black print, if you will.' Trevor smoothed his trouser leg, leaned against his big desk.

I nodded.

'And don't you dare take that off.' He pointed to the necklace that now seemed to be repressing every surge of blood in my throat. I felt light-headed and woozy. It was fear. Nothing more than a surging rush of anxiety at having something pressed to my flesh. Irrational and stupid, but very real to me all the same.

'I won't, Sir.'

He frowned at me.

'Trevor,' I corrected.

'If you are very good, I'll give you a reward tonight.

44

And you're almost always very good, Winona. So I'm not worried in the least.'

I walked out of his office on wonky legs. I felt like I was going to fall, but knew I wouldn't. I took a few deep breaths, making sure to hold them for a count of four in the middle as I'd been taught. It always made me feel better, kept the anxiety at bay some.

Maybe your reward if you behave is he'll add a link to this thing so you can wear it with pleasure ...

I laughed at myself.

* * *

I barely made it to the phone. I was running late and panicking. Trevor would be here in thirty minutes to get me and I was in nothing but black stockings with a garter belt and a black bra. Which I wasn't sure he wanted me to wear.

'Yes, hello, Winona,' I stammered. I forgot if I was in business mode or not. But since I was in my own home, I guessed it didn't matter very much.

'Are you wearing your present?'

'I am.'

'Are you wearing clothes?'

'Technically some,' I said. 'I'm just in here getting dressed.'

'Sit down on the bed.'

I sat.

He wasn't here. He couldn't see me. But I listened and obeyed him as if he were. More for me than for him, I'd realised at some point once upon a time ago.

'Spread your legs,' Trevor said. Then, 'I am assuming you are bare.'

'Yes,' I breathed.

'Open the middle drawer of your nightstand. I want the big black one. The one that's so thick it's hard to get in. I want it set on high. I want it in you before I count to ten.'

There was no room for argument in his orders, but I shifted. 'We'll be late,' I whispered.

'That's one,' he said and my cheeks flushed.

'I'll smell like pussy,' I said, pushing it.

'That's two.' His voice was stony. 'Now then, Winona, you best get moving or I'll have them shorten that neck-lace you're wearing.'

He didn't have to say it twice. I switched on the fat black vibe and it buzzed to life. I turned it to high and heard him chuckle.

'Three,' he said.

I was really wet from the order alone. There was no faking it – Trevor knew me. Just like he knew I longed to call him 'Sir', so he barely ever let me.

The vibrator – smooth, cool black plastic – kissed my clit and I jumped a bit.

'... four ...'

I played it over that thrumming knot of flesh long enough to make me just a touch wetter. Just a touch softer. I panicked a little when he said, '... seven ...' But then I pushed the bent end – angled to stimulate my G-spot – into my slick cunt and sighed.

'Is it in?' His voice was guttural. I could hear the whisper-slide of his hand on his cock as he stroked himself. Or maybe I was imagining it. I liked to think I wasn't.

'It's in,' I gasped.

'Get yourself off twice,' he said. 'And then no panties. I'll be there in fifteen minutes. I'm leaving now.'

And then he hung up. Fear wormed into my gut and amplified my arousal. I came with a loud cry and realised I had fifteen minutes to do it again and then get ready on top of it. So I pushed a finger into my ass, nudging that smooth hot tissue, giving myself just enough pain to get off again – fast and brutal. My preferred method.

I set about wiping myself off with a wet towel to freshen up. He'd said no panties, not no manners.

I put my hair up, minimal makeup, small pearl drop earrings that were set in silver and accented the Claddagh necklace. When the doorbell rang, my stomach trembled and my knees shook a bit. I pulled on my heels, made sure my dress was cinched tight to my waist the way I liked.

At the door Trevor was tall, dark and handsome. Dressed for the party in a smart suit but with a bright-red tie for colour.

'There she is. Did you do as I asked?'

Asked? We both knew that was wrong. Told was more like it.

'Yes.' My voice tried to betray my nerves so I cleared my throat.

'Let's see.' He took three big steps towards me and to keep time with him, I took three big steps back. My ass hit the wall, then my shoulder blades.

Trevor smiled at me. His hand snaked beneath my dress, slid up my leg, slithered over my mound. His fingers pressed to my humid wetness and I felt my eyelids drift shut. 'You're wet.'

I could only nod.

'How many times did you come?' he asked, mouth pressed tight to the curve of my ear.

Nipples painfully hard, voice woefully weak, I said, 'Twice. Once after you hung up and then a few moments later a second time, Sir.'

I bit my lip. I'd done it again. 'Who?' His voice was a sing-song.

'Trevor.'

'I believe you.' His free hand found my throat and pressed the necklace's cool metal to my pulse. I felt the bind of jewellery and flesh and fought to grab a gulp of air.

His hand cupped my mound, palm pressed to my clit, fingers maddeningly close to my slick cunt. I saw sparkles of light in my vision and realised I'd been holding my breath. I inhaled deeply when he plunged his fingers into me, found my G-spot, stroked it masterfully so that my knees went soft and I sagged a little.

'You were a good girl.'

Lips on my temple, lips on my own, lips on the curve of my neck.I surrendered to his soft words and strong hands and came within seconds. Offering him the wet evidence of my pleasure with a soft cry.

'Thank you, Trevor,' I managed, though his hand still caged my throat.

'You're welcome. Let's go.'

When I reached for a tissue to wipe my pussy dry he gave a dismissive grunt. 'Leave it,' he said.

I left it.

It was impossible not to feel the necklace. My fingers plucked and played with it the entire time we were at the party. Trevor's eyes would find me as he schmoozed some man who had millions, maybe billions, of dollars to play with. He'd cock an eyebrow and give me a half-smile as one of his associates would bring me a drink or flirt. Every advance made the necklace feel heavier, as if made of lead instead of a more beautiful and lighter metal.

But, oddly, I also felt safe ... wanted. Possessed. And it inspired a heavy needy heat between my legs. All kinds of bizarre images flashed through my mind. Trevor taking me right there, in the crowded room, for all to see. Simply coming up behind me to flip my skirt up and mount me like some big lion in a grass field. With as much pomp and circumstance as animals mating. Which meant none. A hard, rough, perfunctory fuck in the middle of the teeming, scheming mass of bankers.

My face was hot with the fantasy. My pussy was the same. A small slide of fluid escaped me and my eyes sought him out. He stared me down from about thirtypaces away as if he knew what had just happened. My fingers found the necklace again, sliding beneath it, worrying it. I wasn't sure if I was fussing with it because I wanted it gone, or touching it to make sure it was still there.

He winked at me and, deep inside of me, desperate nerves fluttered, moist internal muscles flexed. God, how I wanted him.

When his one co-worker Max said, 'So how long have you and Trevor been … a couple?' I blushed hotly, gripped the necklace tight.

When I opened my mouth to speak, Trevor's warm voice boomed. 'Long enough.' He touched the necklace from the back, pushing it down enough for it to tighten a hair. For me to feel the constriction. He leaned in close as they laughed, and whispered, 'Property of me,' and kissed my cheek.

The party was winding down and I turned to meet his gaze. 'Please' was all I said.

And then it was a flurry of goodbyes and him hustling me out of there, holding my elbow chivalrously. His big body pressed to mine, me leaching the warmth off him when the winter wind blew up my skirt and made me shiver.

In the car, he cranked the heater. Angled all the vents my way. 'You did very well. Did you have fun?'

'Sort of,' I admitted.

'Nervous?'

I nodded.

'Well, no one would have known it to look at you.' His palm pressed down on my thigh and then slowly moved up. My dress ruched up with the movement like a pleated curtain. Cool winter air mixed with blasting car heat wafted over my thigh, insinuated itself under the fabric of my dress and licked at my wet nether lips. I sighed.

'Good.' Admitting my fear was OK with him. Everything was OK with him.

'I think you deserve a reward, good girl.'

Pleasure flooded me from head to toe, heating the crown of my head, sliding along my skin and bones to puddle in my feet.

He took a left where he should have taken a right to take us to either his house or mine. We ended up at the local park as snowflakes started to sift down from a gunmetal sky shot with navy blue.

'Where are we going?'

'For a walk.'

51

The Boss

It was a stumble and a shuffle in nice heels down a dirt trail. I twisted my ankle a little once and wondered why, in his nice suit and my nice dress, we were in the woods. But I followed.

At the bottom of the slope he turned, pushed me against a towering tree with rough bark that ripped at my dress and my light wool coat. Tore at my hair with cracked rough fingers.

'Hike up that skirt,' he said.

I did it. I hiked up the skirt of my dress with trembling fingers, shaking from nerves and from cold. His fingers were frozen cylinders when they slid into me, swiftly warming to stimulate me to near orgasm.

With a jerk and a sigh, Trevor undid his zipper and lifted my leg to his waist. I was so wet – so utterly wet – that he drove into me easily the next moment. His cock was perfectly warm and perfectly hard. I was full and a small cry burst out of me as he started to move.

'Do you like being my property, Winona?'

'I-I do …' I stammered here, so close to coming I almost forgot myself '… Trevor.'

His hand covered my necklace, driving the metal a little more roughly against the vulnerable spots on my neck. My head went light and fuzzy – with panic more than anything. I was getting enough air; it was the idea of it all that was scaring me.

His hips moved faster and I felt myself clamping down

on him, those internal muscles bunching and gripping – needy wet bits of me, ready to give me an orgasm. Trevor slammed into me so the bark bit my skin, scraped it raw, stung. But I didn't care. The pain added to the pleasure and I cried out, starting to come.

His fingers tightened round my neck, pressing, pressing, pressing the beloved and dreaded necklace to my throat. He growled, 'You can call me Sir. Just for now.'

His hips swung back and forth, back and forth, a flesh-and-blood pendulum delivering stimulation to my nerve endings, and I was coming again, the peak fast and hard and so vicious it rendered me mute.

But finally I managed. 'Sir,' I gasped.

He squeezed my neck a little harder and grunted once, deeply, like an animal, when he spilled into me. We stayed there, frozen under a speckled sky, until I started to shake. It was when he was helping me up the path, holding my hand like a gentleman as his seed slipped out of me with every step, that he said, 'We'll put the necklace away for now. But you can wear it for special occasions.'

Special occasions. Like being shown off. Like being taken in the woods. Like getting to call him Sir. All the things that made my head swim with adrenalin.

'I look forward to it,' I said and followed him out of the woods.

Sole Survivor
Heather Towne

'Did you hear the news?' Angela Martens whispered.

Her colleagues in the payroll department swivelled around in their chairs to look at the excited gossip.

'What news?' Betty Foster, head of the department, asked, a furrow creasing her brow.

Angela pedalled her chair closer to the centre of the group. 'I heard they're going to downsize our department – outsource payroll to an outside company. They're planning to layoff everybody but one employee.'

Phil Keegstra groaned. 'Great. And I just bought a townhouse.'

'Who told you that?' Betty asked sharply.

Angela glanced around, then bent her red head lower, closer. 'Mr Hirsch's secretary, Margie. She heard Mr Hirsch talking about it to the VP of Finance.'

'Are you sure you got it straight?' Felicity Owen queried nervously. She'd just recently got married.

Angela grinned. 'Straight from the horse's mouth – uh, once removed, that is.'

'Who's the one to stay?'

That question came from Lisette Langdon, the newest member of the department. The tall, slender, brown-eyed chestnut brunette had been hired only six months earlier, straight out of high school. She had the least amount of seniority, experience and training, and she knew it. She also knew that wasn't going to stop her from getting where she wanted to go–right to the top. She just hadn't figured out how yet.

Angela glanced at the young woman. 'I don't know. I don't think they've decided yet.'

Betty sniffed and fluffed her dyed-blonde hair. 'Well, as department head, the person who's been here the longest, if anyone is spared, it's sure to be me.'

Nobody made any reply to that comment, everyone lost in their own thoughts. Until Lisette looked up from her long, glossy, red nails and commented, 'What will they need a department head for, if there isn't going to be any department left?'

Betty glared at the woman. The others shifted warily in their chairs, knowing how right Lisette was. Any one of them could stay, or go. They all believed Mr Hirsch, as COO, would be making the fateful decision, but they weren't the least bit sure as to how he'd be making it.

***

Lisette waited until Mr Hirsch's secretary finally went out for lunch. Then she adjusted her top – by popping three more buttons open on the red satin garment. She was wearing the shiny blouse and a pair of black slacks, her brown hair done up, ringlets dangling, face painted with just enough makeup to fully accentuate her high cheekbones and long eyelashes, the sultry depths of her eyes. Her breasts were pushed out and up by a red demi-bra one size too small and, with the blouse buttons undone, were on prominent, plumped porcelain display. She took a deep breath, gripped the 9x12 envelope she'd filched from the mailroom and strolled into Mr Hirsch's office.

The man was bent over some papers on his large mahogany desk. His bald head gleamed under the lights, thick red lips moving along with his pale right hand as he wrote. Lisette glanced at the oil painting of the man's wife and six children up on the wall behind his desk, before fully focusing her attention on Hamish Hirsch, Chief Operating Officer of Consolidated Enterprises, decider of payroll department fates.

Walking up to his desk, she stated huskily, 'Package for you, Mr Hirsch.'

The middle-aged man's lips and pen didn't stop. Despite being the son-in-law of the company's founder and owner, he was a busy man.

Lisette inhaled, pushing her chestwares out even further, and leaned over Mr Hirsch's desk. Her breasts almost spilled out onto his papers. 'Package, Mr Hirsch,' she breathed.

Hamish glanced up into Lisette's blindingly white cleavage. His clear blue eyes registered nothing but annoyance at the interruption. The pair swept up from her pair, onto her pretty face and pursed, puckered lips. 'Stick it in my inbox, please.' He bent his head back down to his work.

Lisette sighed, straightened up and slotted the envelope. She turned to leave.

'Young lady.'

She pirouetted. 'Yes, Mr Hirsch?'

'You should do up your top. You'll catch cold like that.'

***

The next business day, Lisette was wearing a different top–a conservative blue cotton blouse fastened all the way up to the top – and a different pair of slacks: a tight, stretchy white pair that moulded to her taut bottom like they were spray-painted on. The pants split her bum cheeks right down the middle, plunging deep, separating high and wide and out. Her buttocks visibly shifted and shuddered when she walked on her three-inch heels, bum cleavage clefted like there were no pants there at all.

This time, when she brought another envelope in at noontime for the hard-working Mr Hirsch, she fumbled and dropped it on the floor of his office as she attempted to insert it into his inbox. 'Oh, sorry, Mr Hirsch!' she husked, getting his irritated attention.

Then she turned, bent over, almost bursting her young, ripe buttocks right out of the thin seat of her pants. The stretchy material strained to contain the cheeky pair, gone almost sheer with the deep, butt-thrusting bend Lisette was erotically executing right in front of the staring Mr Hirsch.

'Young lady,' Hamish said.

'Yes, Mr Hirsch?' Still bent outrageously over, Lisette craned her neck around to look at the man.

'It's a wonder you don't cut off the circulation to your legs, those pants are so tight.' He bent his head back down to his work.

Lisette sighed and stood up. She slotted the envelope and stalked out of the office.

***

'I know what you're trying to do, honey.' Betty Foster confronted Lisette later that afternoon, as the women sat at their desks. 'We all do.'

'Do what?' Lisette said, not bothering to turn away from her computer screen. If they were all going to be laid off tomorrow except for one, anyway, Betty's authority was moot.

'Shaking your sweet little tits and ass in front of Mr Hirsch,' Betty stated frankly. 'Angela saw you leaving his office at lunchtime the past two days.'

'Did she?'

'Yes, she did. And she saw you drawing a big fat zero for all your slutty efforts, too. You should've done your research, sweetheart – Mr Hirsch is happily married, joyously prolific, religiously devout as Joseph Smith. You could parade around stark-naked on top of his desk, put on a show, and he's just going to tell you to take up square-dancing.'

The others giggled, including Phil.

Lisette punched the keys of her computer with her blood-red fingernails, her butt now almost numb in the super-tight pants. Her belated Internet surfing had confirmed what Betty had just said about the staid Mr Hirsch. 'We'll see,' she replied. 'All men have their weaknesses. You don't get that many children without liking some part of the female anatomy.'

Betty snorted. 'Better try crotchless panties, then, sweetheart, with scripture written on the sides and a cross through your clit. That might get his attention.'

Lisette ignored the laughter. She'd actually thought

about that, but figured that was too much sacrifice for just one lousy accounting position.

***

The next day, payroll doomsday, Lisette Langdon strolled right past Mr Hirsch's secretary and into his office.

'Hey, you can't go in there!' Margie hissed, leaping up from her desk.

Lisette ignored the woman. She didn't even have a package for Hamish this time, just a packaged pair – of legs and feet.

Her red top was done up and her black skirt was short but loose. But her long, lithe, ivory-coloured legs cascaded out from the ruffled hem of the skirt, sheathed in sheer black nylon stockings, pouring down and down in sculpted elegance and eroticism into a pair of red leather, spike-heeled, open-toed shoes strapped to her slim, shapely, platformed feet. Crimson leather tendrils wrapped around her delicate, well-turned ankles, holding the towering shoes in place, highlighting her feet and dizzyingly long legs. Her luxuriant lower limbs whispered seductively together, thighs caressing, four-inch leather heels creaking slightly, as she strolled, hips rolling, legs crossing, tottering just a bit, up to Mr Hirsch's desk.

'I'd like to discuss the layoffs in payroll with you,

Hamish,' she said, stopping two yards in front of the man, so he could see all of her sensually clothed legs and feet.

Margie's fat, angry body crowded the door. 'You can't disturb Mr Hirsch without an appointment!'

Hamish glanced up, annoyed. His blue eyes scanned Lisette up and down, then stuck, wide and unblinking, on the young woman's erotically draped lower limbs, her provocatively packaged peds. 'Uh, th-that's all right, Margie!' he stammered. 'I'll, uh, see her.'

Lisette smiled with relief, then with intent. She fluttered her fingers at Margie, looking up from the stricken man to that family portrait above his desk. She'd only realised it later – as she lay rubbing her pussy in the tub the previous evening, thinking and scheming – that Mrs Hirsch was sitting in the middle of the painted couch, surrounded by her many children, with her long legs crossed, one planted on the ground in a posed, toe-arched position, while the other dangled lithe and gleaming from her knee, both legs and feet bare. That's when she'd discovered the secret to Hamish Hirsch's suck-sex: the way she could make strides in the company.

'Sh-shut the door, please, Margie!' Hamish gasped, bright staring eyes locked on Lisette's perfectly posed stems.

Margie grunted and retreated.

Lisette strutted forwards, journeying long-legged, around Hamish's desk, up to the seated man. He pushed back in his brown leather executive chair and she hit an armrest with the pointed tip of her shoe to spin him around to face her, literally putting her best foot forward. And then putting her foot down–in between the gaping man's legs.

She had nothing to lose now, everything to gain. She'd found Hamish's sexual Achilles heel, and it was attached to her slender foot, and ran all the way up her thirty-inch leg. She pressed the tapered scarlet tip of her shoe downwards, into Hamish's crotch.

He groaned and quivered. His arms hung down on either side of the chair, his legs apart. His mouth was open, his square-shaped face beaming, eyes shiny and glassy. He was looking down at his crotch, at the point of Lisette's shoe pressing on his groin. She could feel his swelling excitement right through the leather.

'Unstrap me,' she breathed, pushing Hamish's bloating erection around.

He looked up at her face, then back down, along her bent leg to her foot. His arms came up, large, hairless hands shaking. His mouth snapped shut and his gulp was audible to Margie in the outer office as he brought his hands together, wrapped trembling fingers around Lisette's leather-twined ankle.

They both moaned.

The man's hands were hot and damp on Lisette's slender ankle, the padded palms pressing right through her stockings, against her bare skin, the blunt fingers curling around. Her pussy tingled, almost fully exposed with her skirt riding up her raised leg.

She wasn't wearing any panties, just red-rosed black garter straps on her toned upper thighs, hooked to the black tops of her stockings and the black belt around her trim tummy. She drew her skirt right up to her narrow waist, showing Hamish her garters, the brown fur of her pussy.

He gripped her ankle, caressed it, winding his fingers round and round, gazing up her one bent stockinged leg at her garters and pussy, down her other straightened stockinged leg. Then back at her foot positioned in between his legs, planted on the pulsating length of his fully engorged cock.

'Unstrap me,' she said again, firmly.

He blinked. Then he fumbled with the red spaghetti straps holding the shoe to Lisette's foot. Somehow he got them unfastened, slowly and shakily unwrapped them from the young woman's ankle. Then he swallowed hard, gripped the back of the shoe, tilted it down and pulled it away from Lisette's black-stockinged foot.

Lisette lifted her foot and her shoe slid off into Hamish's grasping hands.

He watched her bared foot ease away. Until he caught the spicy leather scent of the empty shoe in his hands. And then he pressed his nose into it, against the slim, curved, damp, pale-leather inner sole. He breathed deeply, raggedly, inhaling the musky aroma, his eyes closed rapturously.

Lisette nestled her stockinged foot back down in between Hamish's legs, onto the throbbing lump in his trousers. She pumped her ped, stroking the hardened length of the man's cock, softly gripping it with her toes, gently brushing it with the rounded ball of her foot.

Hamish stuck out his thick pink tongue and licked the naked sole of Lisette's shoe. He tilted the sexy high heel up to his face, holding onto the spike heel and the pointed tip, and dragged his tongue up and down the contoured sole. He rode the wet leather rollercoaster with his outthrust mouth-organ over and over, while Lisette pistoned his cock with her foot.

Her pussy brimmed with sensation as she pushed her foot back and forth on his bulging erection, watching the enthralled man devour her sole. It was powerful, passionate, the once mighty businessman now a plaything for her perfect peds.

She felt his cock surge, spasm under her stroking foot-tip, and she rushed a trembling hand down to her dripping pussy, fingers finding her swollen clit and rubbing. She shuddered and cried out, fired with emotion, her toes locking around Hamish's spurting cock. He grunted and jerked, hot, sticky semen filling his silk shorts and staining his pinstriped trousers, his tongue swirling around the stunning spike heel of Lisette's wanton shoe, lips sucking and sucking and sucking on the hard leather stem.

Lisettepulled her foot off Hamish's spent cock, her

shoe out of his gripping hands. 'So, I'll be the last one standing in payroll, won't I, Hamish?' she said, reheeling.

Hamish's arms dropped back to his sides, limp, his shoulders slumping. 'Actually ... my father-in-law has final say over all personnel decisions.'

Tears misted the man's eyes as he watched Lisette angrily stamp her foot and stride out of his office.

* * *

Powell Clermont, founder and owner of Consolidated Enterprises, had a summer home out in the country. Lisette obtained the address from the employee personnel database after going through Betty Foster's desk and finding the password taped to the underside of a can of mints labelled 'employee database password'.

An hour of twisting country-road driving put her at the black iron front gate of Powell's rural property. A six-foot-high wrought-iron fence guarded the acreage, the white-brick, two-storey house just barely visible from the road through the leafy trees.

Lisette parked on the side of the road and got out of her car. It was a clear, sunny, beautiful day, as days of reckoning often are. The yellow sun beamed down on Lisette's shiny chestnut hair and gleaming white legs. She'd stopped at her apartment to change before heading out, not knowing anything about Powell or *his* preferences.

Now she was wearing the red satin top with the popped-open buttons, the tight white pants converted to tight white shorts, her legs bare, the red leather spike heels strapped to her bare feet. Only six months into the business racket, and she'd already learned efficiency, how to think on your feet–combining tits, ass and legs into one flagrant feminine package. She knew her brains would never get her a place in the country like Powell's, so she used the best of what she had, and she had a lot to offer that powerful men liked.

After scaling the fence with some difficulty, Lisette strode across the emerald expanse of front lawn up to the gleaming red door of the house.

A woman answered the doorbell. 'May I ... help you?' she asked, predatory eyes travelling down Lisette's lusciously clad and exposed body.

'I have important business with Mr Clermont,' Lisette stated.

'I'm his wife, Bernice.' The grey-haired middle-aged woman drew the door closer to her, ready to close it. 'Powell's busy at the moment. Can I give him a message?'

'No message,' Lisette replied tersely, realising she'd never get past the front door. The woman's frumpy dress and sagging body gave no indication as to her quarry's anatomical attribute preferences.

Lisette stepped back as Bernice closed the door in her face. The young woman had seen smoke coming from the chimney of a small building in the backyard of the property, and she knew that where there was smoke, she could start fire. So she ducked under the front window and strolled around the side of the house, into the backyard and over to the building at the rear.

It was the size of a garage, built out of more of the same white brick, a metal overhead door on the side. Lisette knocked on the black wooden door at the front of the building. It was a hot day, and all the exertion had dewed her ivory skin with perspiration, making her face and legs and the rounded portions of her exposed breasts glow.

A man yelled from inside, 'What the hell is it now, Bernice?'

Lisette swallowed, gripped the brass doorknob, turned it and pushed the door open. She walked into the small building, stumbling slightly in her high heels over the lip of the door.

It was a workshop, a single large room with a concrete floor and a beamed ceiling. Woodworking and automotive benches and tools filled the space, and a forge fire burned against the far wall. A man sat on a stool at one of the benches, a wooden dowel in his large hands, a smoking pipe in his large mouth. An unfinished kitchen chair was propped up on the bench in front of him.

He had a full head of silver hair and a silver goatee, a thin, rugged, handsome face, grey eyes, red lips and a

Roman nose, broad shoulders and a lean, muscled body. He looked at Lisette as she threaded her way past the benches and through the scattered wood chunks and car parts to where he sat.

She moved carefully, her large brown eyes locked on his. And she soon had an answer to her burning question: Powell Clermont was staring at her legs, her long, bare, smooth-skinned lower limbs whose lean thigh muscles rippled and sinewy rounded calves clenched as she negotiated the obstacle course and walked up to the top decision-maker at Consolidated Enterprises. She stopped in front of his workbench and planted her stems wide apart, her fists on her hips.

'I work for you, Mr Clermont. And I'm willing to do anything to keep on working for you.'

Powell's wide eyes were glued to the young woman's spread legs. They followed the strident appendages, every erotic clench and ripple, as Lisette suddenly scaled the workbench and stood on her spike heels, towering over the awestruck man with her skyscraper legs.

'Feel them!' she rasped. 'I brought them for you.'

His pipe dropped out of his mouth and clattered to the floor along with the dowel. He lunged forwards, his huge hands shooting out and clamping onto Lisette's slim ankles. She wobbled in the air, realising the intensity of the man's passion for peds and legs as his hands blazed against her bare skin.

Lisette watched, felt, as Powell's damp palms slid upwards, travelling all over her muscular calves, strong fingers roving around the vulnerable soft backs of her knees, hairy hands widening up and onto the vibrating stringed muscles of her thighs. He rose to his feet, gliding his hands up and down the lushest parts of her trembling legs.

It was hot in the room, stuffy. Lisette popped open the button on her shorts, pushed them down off her pussy. He took them the rest of the way, lowering the small garment down her long legs, caressing and stroking and clasping her lower limbs every sensuous inch of the way as he did so. When he finally reached her feet, she lifted her high heels, one at a time, and he pulled her shorts off and flung them away. There were streaks of more than perspiration on Lisette's creamy-white inner thighs, where her pussy had leaked sticky juices.

'Kiss my feet, lick them!' Lisette ordered from her lofty position.

Powell's glittering eyes focused on her feet, erotically arched in the red leather heels. He placed his heavy hands on the humped tops, covering the tender skin, then stroked and petted her peds. He fingered the long, bulb-topped, red-painted toes. Then he bent his silver head down and kissed one arch, then the other.

Lisette shivered from her kissed feet all along the lengthy expanses of her legs. She unbuttoned her top and shrugged

69

it off. She grasped the shimmering mounds of her breasts and squeezed them, slid her slender fingers out to the pointed pink tips and pinched, rolled, as Powell tongued the tops and toes of her feet, licking long and wet and hot.

'Lick your way up my legs, to my pussy!' With the man totally under her control, she would get him to prove his ultimate enslavement—by eating her out.

Powell didn't hesitate. His hands slid back up to the sculpted contours of Lisette's legs. He grasped and groped her stems all over again, adding his lips and tongue and teeth to the erotic skyward adventure, licking around her ankles and along her shins, kissing the hard shells of her knees, biting into the meaty flesh of her thighs. Reaching the dizzying apex of her limbs, he pressed his mouth into the downy brown fur and pouty pink lips of her pussy.

'Yes!' Lisette yelped, unable to control herself.

She deigned to grab onto Powell's bobbing head, sinking her sharp claws into his soft silver hair, as the enthralled man gripped her thighs and lapped her pussy, painting her panting slit with his tongue. He licked hungrily, urgently, anxious to fulfil her command – fulfil her.

Lisette quivered on the end of his stroking tongue, her breasts jumping and legs quaking, pussy and body burning. The man's budded tongue excitedly dragged her engorged clit one too many times, and she shrieked and shuddered, orgasm bursting between her legs and storming through her body and being.

Powell gulped her juices and licked her thighs and pussy clean. Then he looked up at her flushed face for further instructions, his own face shining.

'Take ... take out your cock!' Lisette gasped, still shivering with the aftershocks of all-out orgasm. It was true: there was no greater aphrodisiac than power. 'Sit down! I'm ... going to make you come with my feet.'

Powell yanked his belt open and popped the button on his jeans, tore his zipper and pants down. His cock speared out hard and long and straight, pink shaft smooth and clean-cut, hood mushroomed and purple. He plopped down on his bare ass on the stool, cock eagerly jutting up from his loins.

Lisette licked her lips and shakily sat down on the workbench, limbs bathed in sweat. She stretched her arms out behind her, placed her hands on the scarred surface of the bench, then stretched her legs out in front of her, balancing on her bare bum. She reached out with her toes and clasped Powell's cock.

'Jesus!' he howled, bucking.

Lisette gripped his swollen shaft between her long toes, feeling the throbbing passion of the unabashed legman, her footman. Then she pumped, pulling her legs back, gliding her toes along either side of Powell's cock, then-pushing them forwards again. He bucked again, groaning with pleasure, glaring down at his toed cock.

Lisette pumped faster and faster, her thighs and calves

and feet straining, toes clutching so that the knuckles burned even whiter. Powell's huge cock lengthened and thickened even more between her pumping feet, and pearls of pre-come spilled from the gaping slit at the bloated tip.

Lisette pulled her toes free, flexed them, then grasped Powell's enormous erection between her curved soles and pistoned his cock with her peds. Powell jerked and bellowed. His cock spurted semen, long, thick, leaping hot ropes that splashed Lisette's pussy and rained down on her thighs. The man's eyes flew wildly up and down Lisette's pumping legs, then blazed down at her stroking feet.

Lisette had never seen or felt a man come so hard and so long before. She milked him quivering dry, her legs and pussy coated with his sticky adulation – and capitulation.

***

Lisette wasn't laid off from the payroll department. In fact, Powell promoted her to head of the human resources department. So it became her decision as to who would stay and who would leave.

She put her pampered feet up on her brand-new desk in her new office and crossed her lovely lower limbs. Then did an eeny-meeny-miny-moe with her former co-workers in payroll, applying her good business sense.

Damsel in Success
Rachel Randall

Erin lingers by the stairwell, looking back one last time.

Her leaving party's over. Her former colleagues, eager for a rowdier next round, are waiting for her down at the bar. She's on her way to join them, to toast her leap to the next rung on the corporate ladder. And she will.

Only, there's light flooding from the one office door still ajar.

He's still here. Should she …?

It's tempting to leave without saying goodbye. The old Erin would have left, she knows; cloaked hurt with pride and burned her bridges. She's older and wiser, though, after three years of working with him in this high-pressure environment. She's thrived. Learned to think things through rather than to rely on instinct. And it's clear to her that this *thing* with him needs to be resolved one way or another, once and for all.

She rolls her shoulders to shake out her gathering tension. Not even wine and temporary freedom can remove the weight of unfinished business.

Erin finds Ben standing behind his desk, looking out through the immense glass wall at the back of his office. As always, her first impression of him is one of power worn quietly but well, of competence and a keen mind. She's not sure when it was that she first saw past the good suits and authority of her boss to the man underneath. But since then all she can see is a tall man, with a fit body and a mouth that she has a bad habit of staring at during meetings. A serious man who doesn't take himself seriously – who likes to play squash even though it always makes him hobble the next day, and who's been known to talk Take That with the personal assistants.

He's given her nothing to hang a crush on, has always been perfectly professional, even though she knows better than to think that he hasn't been aware of her interest. Hell, the entire forecasting team knows. But the unspoken rule here is no fooling around with co-workers, and he's never seemed to regret that policy.

Tonight, though, there's clearly something bothering him. His hands are jammed into his trouser pockets, and his neck is rigid as he watches something out on the street. From this angle, she can see every detail of his reflected face – the strong frames of his glasses, the thoughtful set of his jaw. The sudden tilt of his head when he notices her watching him.

They stand like that for a moment, watching each other in the glass, before he says, 'Spectacular, isn't it?'

Her heels click, too loud, on the floor as she crosses to join him. The City, spread out below them, is lit up against the wintry evening. Streaming white headlights, stuttering red brakes. The dome of Liverpool Street Station, glowing like a commuter beacon. And at the farthest left-hand corner, majestic St Paul's and a hint of river where the lights refract on the water.

'Oh, yes.' She turns away from the view because it's just too hard not to keep looking at him instead.

There's paperwork on his desk, haphazardly strewn and abandoned. Erin wonders what he's working on so late that's making him frown, and that has kept him only briefly and at the periphery of her farewell drinks.

That's none of my business any more, she reminds herself sternly.

When she can't resist glancing back at him, she sees that he's still looking distracted.

'So,' he says. 'You're off to wreak havoc on some other poor sod.'

'I've got a few weeks' leave first,' she tells him, grinning at this flash of humour from him. It's moments like this that made her fall for him, she knows; a mentor with a naughty streak. Erin wonders if that's why they've always got along so well – she's always been a student with sass.

He nods. 'Smart idea,' he says. 'Always best to start something new with a clear head. This place can be hard to shake off.'

'Some things about it, anyway,' she agrees, daring him to bite.

His raised brows make it obvious he's seen the bait. 'We haven't had much time to discuss your new job,' he says, eluding her again. 'How hard did you have to push them to get the deal you wanted?'

'It was a good offer.'

His gaze sharpens. 'You didn't negotiate?'

Flummoxed, still thinking about what it might take to wear down his resistance, her reply is the shade of vague that she knows from experience acts as a red flag to the mentor in him. 'Well … all the details aren't quite sorted yet.'

'Erin, make sure that you negotiate. *Always* negotiate. Every thousand you start on will mean hundreds of thousands over the course of your career. Quantify why you're worth more than their initial offer, and think about what you want in terms of flex-time, holiday, bonuses.' He scowls into the distance, not so much at her as at some imagined Human Resources lackey. 'You should be walking into this with at least a company car.'

This side of him is so familiar, so comfortable, that

she finds herself instinctively looking around for the chair she usually sits in when she's taking notes in meetings. She catches herself just in time – I don't work for him anymore, she reminds herself – and shakes her head. 'I'll handle it.'

The words sound defensive rather than assured, and she grits her teeth as Ben gives her a searching look. He glances down at the digital clock beside his computer. Light from the desk lamp picks out a few strands of silver amid the dark gold of his hair. 'It's late. I assumed you'd be going out to celebrate.'

It's a dismissal, and it stings. She swallows her pride and her retort. If this is the last time she'll be in his office, she wants to make sure he knows how much she's appreciated her time here. 'I am,' she says. 'I just wanted to say thank you. And goodbye.'

She holds out her hand and, to her surprise, he takes it in both of his. She can feel his thudding pulse, tickling her fingertips. She shivers as they hold like that, all her prickliness melting away. Without looking she knows that her nipples must be visibly hard. Reluctantly, she draws her hand away and her skin buzzes in the aftermath of his touch.

'Goodbye, Erin,' he says, seemingly unaffected. 'Best of luck with your future endeavours.'

She can't read his expression, but it's the same look he'd worn when she'd given her recent presentation to the Board. Then, it had been unnerving to have no idea what was going through his head. Now, she just feels disappointment.

'So. We ... we're at the All Bar One if you'd like to join us when you're finished here.'

He doesn't reply, so she straightens her pencil skirt, giving him time, hoping he'll take the opportunity. His mouth is parted slightly, but his eyes have gone distant. *Right, then.*

'Bye,' she says, reluctantly turning her back on him.

'Erin,' he calls out suddenly. 'A word of advice, before you go.'

She pauses a step away from the door, held in place by the challenge she recognises in his voice. The same tone she's come to associate with him setting her an assignment that punched above her weight.

'Learn to ask for what you want, or you'll never get it.'

Erin whirls to see him leaning forwards with hands planted against the desktop. Incredibly, she hears her own desire in his tone. She steps towards him, shoulders squared, chin up, drawing encouragement from the way his eyes gleam back at her.

'My life is not a teaching exercise!'

'No,' he counters. 'But you obviously need advice.'

'I'm not the same girl you took a chance on, Ben,' she warns him. Frustration makes her voice waver. 'I've earned my way and I'm not looking for advice.'

'I know what you're looking for.' He says it with the same casual certainty he'd once said, 'The projections for Q4 are off, do them again,' and 'I'm sure you'll be an excellent addition to our team, Ms Ross,' but his phrasing is so sexual that, for a moment, she can scarcely believe it.

Then the excitement kicks in. 'The reference you wrote for me,' she says, riding the adrenalin. 'What did you say?'

'That you were extraordinarily capable. That you have ambition, and that I fully expect to see you achieve great things. And while your inexperience occasionally betrays you, you learn from your mistakes. I said,' her former boss tells her, 'that I'm constantly impressed by your professionalism.'

She recognises the teasing jibe for what it is, but she's too overwhelmed by the rest to respond. 'That's –' she swallows, her throat dry '– very generous.'

He smiles at her. His mouth is beautiful; mobile and lush. How many times has she thought about that mouth on her body? Too many times not to give this a serious try, she tells herself.

Determination gives her the impetus to continue. 'And what would you say to me, if you could say anything? What would *that* reference say?'

He focuses on her with all the interest she's ever wanted from him. The heat of his full attention scorches.

'I'd tell you that you've come a long way, but that you still need to separate doing a good job from doing a good job *for* someone. I'd tell you that being good isn't enough and that you need to learn how to negotiate, so you get what you deserve. I'd tell you that when you're sitting in my office, being clever, it makes me want to pull you across this desk, push your skirt up and fuck you until you can't remember anything but my name.'

'Ben –'

'I'm telling you now. I'll be very, very sorry to see you walk out that door.' She closes her eyes for a moment, savouring it all but uncertain as rules shatter around her. She breathes deeply before meeting his gaze. 'Maybe I do need some guidance,' she says.

He crooks his finger, beckoning her closer. She considers him, drawing out the moment, before she stalks forward. There's more swing in her hips than she's ever used during office hours, and as a statement of intent it does the trick. When she reaches for his tie and winds the silk around her fist, she's gratified to see the swift rise and fall of his chest as his breathing quickens.

There's a slight tremor in her voice as she says, 'I want to get what I deserve, Ben.'

It's enough to satisfy him for now, thank God, because he kisses her like he can't wait a moment longer.

It's good, Erin thinks, to know that it isn't only her, that she hasn't been alone in this for so long. Even if she wants to bloody kill him for making her wait. Her mouth is tingling and her knees feel weak. 'An office romance,' she murmurs against his lips. 'I don't want to get into trouble with my boss.'

His smile is slow and predatory as he rests on the edge of the desk. It ignites her lust, makes her body clamour for more attention. Kissing him again has taken on a compelling urgency. She lets him pull her between his thighs, until her trembling knees hit the underside of the desk.

His hands skim up her hips, following the darts on her Thomas Pink shirt to frame her waist. He splays his fingers and rubs gently through the fabric. 'You don't work for me any more,' he reminds her. 'Though I do hope you'll consider offering me freelance services.'

She gasps as he strokes a sensitive spot. 'You have something in mind?'

Laughter crinkles the corner of his eyes. 'Just keeping you busy until you start your next job.'

She laughs back at him, feeling happiness rise like a bubble in her chest. It seems very natural to take off his glasses and set them aside in preparation. 'What, in bed?'

'Unless you have a better offer.'

His hands are so warm, just as she's always imagined, but his mouth isn't soft at all. He pushes against her, demanding, his fingers digging into her ribs as his tongue slides past her lips.

She's tried so hard not to romanticise. But yes, she's imagined this, and yes, it's a thousand times more amazing, more dirty, more *everything* to kiss him here in his office, in real life. It's as empowering as it is embarrassing to want to give like this, to need to take like this.

She pours all these contradictions into their kiss. Lets him stroke across her teeth, her tongue, then pushes back and grasps his jaw with her hands so she can hold him at the perfect angle. She draws back only when she needs to breathe. They're both panting, already on fire for each other.

'Stay there,' she tells him, pressing her fingertip to his lips. He does it —staying still and silent, watching her with eyes gone dark as she kicks off her heels and shimmies out of her skirt and stockings. She unbuttons her shirt slowly enough to make him twitch, his obedience gone the way of impatience.

'Come back here,' he demands. His trousers have drawn tight across his thighs and groin, and the ridge of him presses, tantalising, against his front zip.

She resists an instant longer. 'Just considering my options.'

When she's wearing only her black knickers and bra, Erin presses him backwards, letting her momentum flatten him to the desk. Papers fly off onto the floor, but spreadsheets are the last thing she's thinking about.

'So,' she muses as she rakes a hand through her kiss-dishevelled black hair. 'The position is appealing.' She straddles his hips. 'I'd like to know more about the

compensation you have in mind. Tell me about your –'
she squirms down against him, grinding into the hard
bulk of him beneath the fine worsted '– package.'

He barks out a chuckle even as his hips surge upwards.
Somewhere in the heady rush of overwhelming *contact*,
she falls onto him, her curves melting into his angles.
Erin tilts back just a bit, letting him see her want for him
written all over her face. Their mouths smash together in
a kiss that's messy, slippery, but barely enough to satisfy.

Ben shoves his body more tightly against hers so she
feels every rigid inch of him. The yielding folds of her
pussy begin to mould to his shape, even through the
barriers of fabric. His shirt is damp with perspiration
and the musk-and-sex scent of him makes her salivate.
She suddenly wants to get his cock into her mouth,
desperately. He feels thick, hot, blunt underneath her. She
wants that in her body, working her. Testing her limits.

'Too many clothes,' she mutters, working down his
zipper.

He bucks up, nearly dislodging her.

She licks across the day's stubble roughening his chin.
'*Definitely* too many clothes,' she rasps. 'Take them off?'

His hands tangle in her hair, pulling, but his gaze is
fixed on the fullness of her breasts as they press against
his chest. 'I'm afraid that offer's not on the table yet.'

He twists up, then rolls them over and off the desk.
Sharp corners dig into her hip, making her cry out in

surprise. She barely notices that her feet have hit the floor and that Ben is frogmarching her across the room.

She's still blinking back tears of shocked pain when he pushes her against the window, his hips and chest pinning her easily. The plate glass is cool on her belly, her breasts, the tops of her thighs; his hands are deliciously rough on her ass, the long line of her back, the nape of her neck.

Erin slaps her palms against the glass, but she's going nowhere – and she doesn't want to. Everywhere around her London glows, and, trapped against this panorama of power and money, all she wants is the man right here with her. She knows it would be easy, very easy, to flatten her cheek against the glass, to close her eyes and enjoy the ride. But while this man has taught her patience, with her body craving every sensation she can get, she's not about to wait for his lead.

Her eyelids flutter at the proximity of her own reflection. I look naughty, she thinks. Off my head with lust. She loves it. Cars blur far below, the afterburn of their neon passing scorching across her retinas. Her hands skid wider, their skin as slick and hot as the restless ache between her thighs. From here, she can see the sign for the bar on the corner where the office crew are waiting. Anyone might come back looking for her, find them together. Thrilled panic spins her even higher.

'More,' she breathes, the syllables smudging against the pane.

His face is still jammed up close to hers, his breath damp at the shell of her ear. His mouth parts and her pulse trips out the time for every second of silence. But, instead of speaking, he slants his lips down the side of her throat, sucking hard to bring blood surging to the surface. Pleasure cuts through her, a line from his working mouth right down to the nerve endings in her swelling clit.

'Don't mark me.' It's a token protest.

He worries his teeth against her skin as if to confirm that he knows her demand is far from heartfelt. 'I'm willing to compromise so you get what you want,' he rumbles, 'but you're going to have to give a little back here.'

She can hardly *think*, can barely stand still. 'Do it then,' she urges him.

Without hesitation, he bites down lightly into the meat over her collarbone. She cries out, shifting anxiously against his body and thrusting her ass back into his hips. 'Hard, please, harder.'

Finally, *finally* slipping his fingers between her legs, he finds her sopping knickers and yanks the cotton down so he can massage her already plump folds. Fresh slickness coats her pussy, making them both groan. She can feel the heated pressure of his mouth on her skin all the way down to her sex.

'Harder –'

He curses, and *sucks*, pinching her clit between his

thumb and finger as he does it. The shock of it sends the first little explosion rocking through her.

'You're supposed to negotiate,' he reminds her, 'not make unreasonable demands.' He skates his fingers back across the seam of her pussy, easing out more moisture.

Erin wriggles around in the circle of his arms so she can see him. He has to stop touching her when she moves, but the sight of him is almost as intoxicating. His mouth is reddened, his cheeks flushed. Once perfect hair skews across his forehead, and without his glasses on he's squinting slightly to keep her in focus. His pupils are huge, spread wide and vulnerable. The boss, debauched, she thinks, and feels her power.

He's stroking his palm down her spine. When he closes his other hand across the back of her neck and squeezes gently, she lets out a reedy moan.

'Condom?' he murmurs, pressing his lips to her forehead. His squared-off fingernails scratch at her nape.

She waves at the floor by the door where she'd dropped her handbag.

His hand stills even as his breathing quickens. 'Showing that six-figure initiative.'

While he's gone, she crosses dreamily to the window, trailing her fingertips along it as she chooses a place to settle. Her orgasm is still tingling through her, insulating her from everything but *Ben*.

Behind her she hears the crinkle of foil and the sound

tightens her nipples, her belly. His groan of pleasure as he strokes on the rubber is unrestrained. The sound travels through her, and it seems utterly sensible to lean into the window again, ready for him.

She feels the heat of his body first, counterpoint to the chill of the glass. Then comes the shock of his bare chest against her back, as the edges of his now unbuttoned shirt tickle her ribs. 'Yes,' she hisses, and shuts her eyes, pushing out her ass towards him.

His fingers hook into her knickers and he yanks them down around her ankles. He's crowding her, holding her hips, rubbing against her skin. She wants to turn around like she had before, to see him bare and ready for her. Later, she promises herself, her thoughts feverish. Later she'll sink to her knees right in front of him and see and taste all that she wants of his cock. Right *now* she wants him inside her, and her body won't let her interrupt again.

Erin's palms slide in an uncontrolled arc at the first heavy nudge of his cock against her pussy. Her cheek flattens against the window. The angle's awkward; her shoulder burns in protest. Pinioned between his strong body and the fragile glass separating her from the night, she's hypersensitive to every inch of him as he pushes into her. She claws at the glass, mindless with him. The sensation of falling is almost unbearable and the insistent pressure of his cock is her only anchor. This is worth it, she thinks wildly, anything, *anything* –

'Yeah?' Ben mutters into her hair. His fingers move erratically over her skin, and she realises with a thrill that he's touching the place where he'd marked her.

'Yeah,' she moans back at him, and that's all the confirmation he seems to need to grab her harder. He *shoves*, holding her in place. Riding her up onto the very tips of her toes. Deep waves of pleasure make her clench around him. They groan in unison as he keeps her there, balanced on the edge, while he rocks against her.

She closes her eyes, unable to bear visual as well as physical stimulation. Her breasts feel full and ripe; lights spark behind her eyelids. Between their frantically rubbing bodies, sweat pools hot then spills down over overheated skin.

Erin reaches between her legs, seeking him. Her rubbing fingers brush the soft skin of his full sac, and his groan vibrates all the way down her spine. She can feel the tension gathering in his muscles already, the trembling of his thighs. It's filthy, the way she can feel him moving into her like this. It drives her right to the edge.

She bends forwards, making it easier for him to clamp hands onto her hips and draw her to him. Fast and deep, long and hard. Over and over again, until the friction of him is good, so *so* good –

Ben suddenly holds very still, his breath sawing as he begins to come. He shudders, pulsing into her. His weight drapes across her back, heavy, and her hands make sympathetic fists against the glass until, with a sigh of pleasure, he slowly pulls out. Her juice trickles down her inner thigh; she feels the sticky heat and thinks again about sucking him, of tasting herself on his glistening cock.

She's lost in that fantasy, still close to coming herself, when he spins her around and pushes her into the position he wants. Nudging between her legs, Ben half-lifts her with hands underneath her ass. When he jams his thigh up against her needy pussy, she wraps her arms around his neck and gratefully rubs herself off across his hair-roughened skin.

'*Erin*,' Ben urges, hitching her higher.

Pressure builds then implodes, and she can only hook her leg around his waist, unable to speak as she grinds out her orgasm. He doesn't even give her time to recover before he's picked her right up in his arms and laid her back down on the desk. He brackets her body with his, and kisses her. He tastes like sex and salt, and the bitterness of too many coffees.

'I feel amazing,' she tells him when she finally catches her breath. And she does: every inch of her skin feels alive. Flushed and energised ... and ready to go again as soon as possible.

'Winning your negotiations will do that.' He grins down at her with an expression that, for once, is perfectly readable. Half hunger, half humour – he's letting her know that he's ready to clear his schedule for whatever she's planning.

And yes, she has *ideas*.

'Best of luck with your future endeavours?' she mimics, her nails digging into his back until he gasps.

'You're right,' he says. 'Insulting.' The words are damp against the hollow of her throat. He licks her there until she gasps back. 'We've still to discuss your benefits,' he reminds her. 'Can't have anyone taking advantage.'

Smiling up at the ceiling, she stretches to give him more of her to play with. She thinks about what they'll do later, at his place or hers. The way she's going to negotiate all his clothes off again, and then have him naked against her in bed so he can fuck her till she's screaming. She wonders what his initial offer will be, and how soon she'll counter-offer the lavish blowjob she's planning. But why not take the initiative right from the start?

She smirks up at him. 'I want you. Again. Now. Or I walk.' She shrugs innocently. 'Sometimes I just don't feel like making concessions over the important points.'

He eyes her. 'We've unleashed a madwoman here. You never really needed my help at all, did you?'

'Probably not. But feel free to make me any offers you like.' She grabs his tie, yanking him closer so she can whisper her next words directly into his ear. 'I promise I won't make you wait *too* long before I'll say yes.'

Charming the Boss
Olivia London

Not a day goes by when Elena Carlton doesn't feel like a throwback to a less tendentious time in history. She simply wasn't made for competition; she was always more comfortable being acted upon and done for. She would accept the milestone of the big three-oh with the knowledge she couldn't possibly change a tyre or enjoy dining at a restaurant alone. It was a thrill when she finally mastered the art of boiling an egg.

As beautiful as she was and thoroughly lacking in ambition, it was her dire luck to be born working class; a woman of her sort needs a trust fund. But, lacking this essential, she tried making her way in the world while keeping the door open for a little help.

Elena had grown up in Florida, 'the pawn your jewellery state' as she liked to call it, and seized the first opportunity to leave. That opportunity came when, at the age of nineteen, a pizza-dough salesman lured her away from her waitressing job at Tino's, Tampa's only Italian restaurant, to help him with a gourmet pie establishment in San Francisco.

So she said goodbye to too much sunshine and put her trust in the hands of Vic, a salt-and-pepper-haired, silver-tongued lothario sixteen years her senior.

Vic offered to front the rent for a swank apartment but her stomach went queasy at that one. Instead, she found cheap digs in the Haight-Ashbury neighbourhood, renting a flat with an art student named Peg. Elena worked constantly and Peg spent every spare moment with her musician boyfriend so the two young women got along just fine. Outside of stray cats caterwauling in the alley and a neighbour who went through life wearing housecoats and watching endless television shows with the volume turned to its utmost stentorian level, the place was perfect.

She bought a scooter to motor around the city as driving a car gave her road rage. Vic didn't like her living so far from the job but he never asked her to move in with him. He said he was estranged from his wife, mumbled something about divorce and intoned that he just wasn't ready to settle down again.

El could accept that. She was at the start of her life – her real life, as Florida was just a blur now – and she crested towards every peak and thrill of adventure.

The Bay Area's North Beach neighbourhood vaunted so many places to enjoy authentic cuisine that she was rarely homesick for her mother's marinara. And Vic was a great boss. Every time he sent her out on an errand he told her to take her time and keep the change. She loved watching him work a room. He could have been an august statesman in ancient Rome or a cravat-wearing film producer. Instead, he was a charismatic purveyor of pasta and calzones, the man to go to if you wanted to know about sauce.

He had big dreams, as so many culinary kings do. Vic wouldn't rest until he got his mug on the home cooking channel and convinced American housewives a meal just wasn't a meal unless it was served *al pomodoro*.

Vic and his star employee would take frequent trips to Napa Valley wine country, where they purchased the best reserve vintages for upcoming banquets. Once, Vic even treated El to a hot-air-balloon ride and she knew that must have cost a packet. When her boss mentioned above-ground flights were the discovery of eighteenth-century French aristocracy, she tried to imagine what yesteryear's Francophones would think of today's tourists capitalising on their art. It would have them reaching for the nearest bottle of Chambord, surely.

Fall was fast becoming El's favourite time of year. It was certainly the best time of year to be young and living in the Bay Area. In September, after a few grand tours of wineries and much anticipated wine tastings, El didn't balk when her boss said he'd booked a room for them in one of the quainter bed and breakfast inns. The sexual tension between them had been climbing steadily like a Russian vine and, away from work and the bustle of customers, they were able to conduct their lovemaking in earnest.

Elena was every man's dream girl. She was a firm believer in fellatio for breakfast, loving nothing more than the sight of a hard-on in the morning. The morning after the balloon-ride extravaganza, she burrowed under the percale sheets to give Vic's cock a ride of its own. She let her tongue caress the tip of his cockbefore zigzagging it down to his scrotum; then, using her palm as a net, she cupped his cobs with one hand while using her other to guide his magnificent shaft down her throat. She sucked him greedily until he was about to erupt and then he straddled her so he could come on her nipples and belly, his hot semen tickling her skin as she writhed and sighed from the satisfaction.

She wanted only to please. Was that so wrong? She loved the way she felt when she was with him. Some days, her boss made her feel as substantial as meat-loaf, relying more and more on his second-in-command for advice regarding décor, menu offerings and the ever delicate task of hiring and firing bartenders and servers. Other days, she could have been the powdered sugar on a hot cross bun, so light and airy as he picked her up by the waist and twirled her round and round after a particularly successful day.

Life was good and she thanked the lucky alignment of stars that brought her to this delicious fate.

She never pressured Vic about their future but, as more and more shady characters moved into her building, she started to wonder what it would be like to have a stabilised home. She brought the matter up one early afternoon as her boss was shaping flat tyres of dough into what would eventually be focaccia bread drizzled with olive oil then sprinkled with salt.

Vic sighed. 'Elena, you've been great. It's just – well, I've been meaning to tell you … my wife and I got back together. She found out about us and I have to let you go.'

Elena nodded. She reached into her pocket for a scrunchie to pull back her long blonde hair. Her mind was already wandering to a certain bakery on Columbus whose focaccia and cappuccinos rivalled what she'd grown accustomed to at work.

'I'm famished. Mind if I eat?'

Vic smiled at the rhetorical question. He was never one to let an employee go hungry.

Elena worked out the week and collected her pay, which included a bonus to tide her over until she found another job. She and her former boss parted as friends and she quickly found work at one of the big hotels in Union Square. She was remarkably calm about her situation.

While she was quite fond of Vic, she had to admit she wasn't in love with him so there could be no real future for them. Still, it was mighty fun while it lasted.

She eventually found an affordable apartment in Noe Valley that was close enough to Market Street to catch a bus to and from downtown. Now, her backyard was a love nest for raccoons; the only cats she saw were fluffy butterballs perched on windowsills, eyeing passers-by with cheeky insouciance. She didn't know how long she could live among the DINKS – the Double Income No Kids set seemed to sense in her a cautionary tale: a single woman with no real direction in life. Well, at least she wasn't doing anything illegal.

El had great difficulty finding her niche. She made numerous attempts to obtain a college degree but she wasn't exactly a wonk. She went from job to job and she had to admit the only thing she was really good at was the enjoyment of sybaritic culture.

She didn't know how it happened but one day she turned thirty and she was still working as a banquet server. On her lunch break she was flipping through a recent issue of the *San Francisco Charmer*, a free weekly tabloid where employers placed the most unconventional 'help wanted' ads.

She decided she would give the Bay Area one last chance. If she couldn't find her calling, she'd pack her bags and move back to Florida.

And that's when she met Declan Donohue. Mr Donohue owned a condo in Pacific Heights and he asked El to meet him at a coffee shop on Fillmore. He was wearing a business suit and she immediately felt underdressed, having shown up in jeans and a hoodie.

He smiled at her embarrassment. 'It's OK. I told you to dress casual. Remember?'

She gulped and nodded, trying not to openly stare. He was so handsome! How could she possibly get through this interview without making a fool of herself?

'Ahem, let's get started. If your résumé is authentic, it's apparent you have no career objectives. You hold no degrees and you've never worked a job that didn't require you to wear an apron or a nametag. Is this information correct?'

El gulped again. 'Um, yes. That is absolutely correct. I'm not exactly driven. I like to eat, drink and merrily pursue what life has to offer for free. To be perfectly honest, I wish I didn't have to work, but, since I do, I'd like to find something not too stressful.'

'Great! You're hired. I need a factotum, not an MBA. I want someone who will stick around. Like I said in my ad, I write mysteries and science fiction novels. Sometimes I do a little ghost writing. I just need someone to file, organise my notes, run to the post office for me and not complain about making coffee. Can you start today?'

El looked around to see if this was a joke; maybe she was being filmed for some silly reality-TV show.

'Sure, Mr Donohue.'

'Declan, please.' He shook her hand and when Elena felt his skin on hers it was the equivalent of being faradised on the spot. She didn't care if this bespectacled gent wrote books for a living. She was going to fuck this man until his brainpan rattled. It was only a matter of time.

Pacific Heights is one of the city's few low-density neighbourhoods, so, as they strolled back to the boss's place, the occasional bird could be heard warbling when their conversation lulled.

Elena's family was blue-collar; she never felt comfortable around intellectuals. But this man went out of his way to put her at ease. He told her about all the crap jobs he worked to put himself through school. And he seemed to genuinely find her lack of vocation charming.

'You just need to make a list of all the things you're passionate about. What are some of the things you like to do?'

'Well, I know a lot about food and wine, but that doesn't mean I have a passion for the culinary arts. I just fell into catering because I grew up around good food. And you can tell by my figure I like to eat. Let's see. Took some drawing classes at art school only to be told I'm not the next Picasso. Went to massage school only to realise, if I'm holding a bottle of almond oil, somebody's going to get a handjob.'

98

Donohue put his hands up in mock arrest. 'OK, here we are. I'm sure I can find some honest work for you to do.'

El was immediately impressed by the wall-to-wall books but there wasn't much time to gawp. Her new boss presented her with an ergonomic chair at a mahogany desk and gave her a stack of handwritten notes he wanted transferred to a twenty-first-century format.

After two hours of transcribing, she was startled by a rattling sound made by a cup and saucer. Her boss had just handed her some much needed fuel.

'If you don't mind, I'll make the coffee too, sometimes.'

Don't jump him yet, Elena warned her randy self. Don't scare him.

Just a week after working in Pacific Heights, Elena had forgotten what it was like to wear an apron all day and come home at night reeking of garlic. She could get used to this genteel setting. She didn't mind the factotum work if it meant being privy to the warm, wonderful scent of Declan's cologne. The timbre of his dictation reached her ears like the voice of an angel. She constantly imagined raking her fingers through his thick black hair and kissing his sweet, handsome face. She feared his reaction if he knew how wet she was in her seat while trying to retain an erect carriage.

Maybe he'd fire her. One never knew if a man of letters had a libido.

A fortnight into her new gig, she was so frustrated that there was nothing to do but go home and masturbate. As she made ready to leave, having piled her boss's notes in an organised fashion, she pulled a book from her purse and returned the paperback to its rightful place on the mantel.

Running his fingers through the ebony hair El coveted, Declan paused under an archway and said, 'That's an early one. Did you enjoy it?'

'Yes,' she admitted. 'Almost forgot I was reading science fiction.'

'Ha! Well, thanks for everything. See you tomorrow, then.'

Elena took a deep breath. She had to make a move or forever file her lust.

'Is there anything else I can get you before I leave? Some stamps from the post office? Coffee? A blowjob?'

Declan let out a low whistle and shook his head ruefully. 'This isn't that kind of job, El.'

'I know,' she said, walking towards him to unzip his fly. 'I have boundary issues. I'm sorry, but I have to do this. I have to love you up; I just have to.'

Once Declan's cock was released to the flagrant world, El held it in her palm, caressing the erection, lightly waiting for her boss to demur.

He looked at her and smiled. The time for taking umbrage had passed. He would accept the heat of her desire and, even if he didn't wish to see her again, she would forever warm herself with the memory of the moment.

His cock thrilled to her touch, bounding out of her hands and into her mouth. With her glossa as adept, she could have charmed his wand from the depths of an Ali Baba basket. She let her tongue loll round the crest before making exquisite progress down to the root of his shaft, compressing her lips there so the entirety of his maleness would feel wholly and completely loved.

Declan murmured words of appreciation as El's lips took pulls back up to the tip of his cock, where she let her tongue knead and pleasure that heavenly lobe. His hands ranged over her nape and the crown of her blonde head as she licked and loved and licked and loved, learning at long last what it meant to go weak in the knees.

He nearly buckled from the weight of the ecstasy she was handing him on a golden platter but, when she gormandised his phallic offering with pure, uninhibited deep throat, he froze in place, riveted. When he came, she felt cleansed and spirited, his semen the closest thing to a balm her soul could approve.

And so the two enjoyed a tectonic shift in their work relationship. Every day before she went home, El would make lingual love to Dec's cock. It wasn't something that needed to be addressed; it was just something that needed to happen.

Sometimes she'd give him a massage and then fixate on fellatio. Other times she'd cradle his cock in her palm and hold it there so long Dec assumed that day he'd only be getting a handjob. He'd be wrong. She was just treating his maleness like an *objet d'art* before welcoming the wondrous pulse of him to her palate.

One day, after she had gone down on him and pleasured him to the point where he thought he might burst, he slipped his hand down her panties and finger-fucked her until she came.

'You're so wet,' he whispered in her ear. 'All this from going down on me.'

El shrugged. 'Making you happy is the biggest turn-on. The approval in your eyes is the greatest aphrodisiac.'

Declan made no reply to that. Instead he took her out to dinner to a crowded trattoria where the din made intimate conversation impossible.

One of the many things El liked about her boss was how generous he was with his knowledge. He let her borrow books and trade publications, Xeroxed articles for her to take home and even fronted membership fees so she could join the PFW.

The Prodigious Fellows Well-Endowed Library was a private lending library in the Financial District. She never knew such a thing existed – it didn't seem right somehow, paying to use a library – but she was touched Dec thought the likes of her could benefit from such a place. She tried to calibrate her reading by checking out one weighty tome for every five popular fiction novels. Not a bad ratio for a woman whose career objective was yet to be determined.

One blustery afternoon, as Elena was clutching a handful of books having just left the PFW, she bumped into Victor Tollorino, her former boss and mentor.

He was looking unethically tan for this time of year, a chill grey day in February when Bay Area bibliophiles were either wan and harried, hunched over a stack of papers or home with a nice cup of cambric tea.

'Elena, baby!' Vic embraced his erstwhile employee then stepped back to give her a look-over.

'El, you're lookin' good. How many years has it been? Six? Seven?'

'Nine, Vic. Nine years have passed and I still don't have a career.'

Why did she have to say that? She suddenly felt naked on the sidewalk, baring her foibles for the whole world to see.

'Well, then, this is a happy coincidence. I just opened a joint in San Diego. You'd love it there. They got some famous zoo; you were crazy about animals as I recall.'

'Um, I don't have a career but I do have a job.'

'Hey, c'mon. Let's get out of this wind. Go have a drink or something.'

'I can't. My heart belongs to someone. It wouldn't be right.'

103

Vic flashed his most toothsome smile. 'Good for you, kid. Your fella wouldn't object to you having coffee with an old friend. C'mon.'

And so they sat in a well-lit café and talked about the challenges of peddling pasta in a city where more and more people were demanding low-fat, low-carb meals.

She noticed he wasn't wearing a wedding band but decided not to enquire about his marital situation. It was none of her business. Not anymore.

'So, what do you say, El? You could run your own show in San Diego. Book the entertainers, plan the menu. San Fran's not the place for an aging slacker, hon.'

El stood up. 'I'm not moving. I'm in love.' And as soon as she said the words she knew it was true: she was madly in love with Declan Donohue.

'Goodbye, Vic. Good luck with your new restaurant.'

She turned on her heels and made haste to Pacific Heights where Declan greeted her at the door with her third cappuccino of the day and a lengthy to-do list.

She sped merrily through her work, looking forward to her reward: ladles of kisses followed by a rich serving of fellatio. She also had some good news she wanted to share but that was just a strawberry in the shortcake. First, she wanted to sup on what her palate most craved.

El had only managed to savour the tip of Dec's cock and a few languid trips to the base of his shaft when the erudite man pulled her to her feet and changed the scenery.

He had always kept his bedroom door closed, but today he opened it and helped her out of her clothes until she was completely naked.

His fingers dovetailed between her thighs and he groaned at the warm welcome he found there.

'Do you want me to make love to you?' he asked, even as he parted her legs and pinned her to the chenille counterpane.

'I've wanted you from the day we met.' Before he entered her, she risked adding, 'I've waited for you all my life.'

He looked deeply into her eyes and smiled. The risk had been worth taking.

As the tip of his cock probed her opening, she wished in vain she had never lain with another man. Some would say Elena Carlton had had more than her fair share of sex, but with Declan she was finally ready to make love.

I love you, Dec. I love you, I love you, I love you. She mentally shouted these words to the roof beams as their bodies rocked in tandem with this new blessed sense of purpose. His cock inside her was a beacon lighting her on the road to rapture, each thrust making her vulva more pliant, her loins two trembling boughs in a carnal storm.

She wanted to be loved by him, fucked by him. Taken, broken and put back together again. For the first time in her life she felt whole.

She came in uninhibited volleys of pleasure and, after love, they spooned together for a long while, both happy to rest in the lee of love's embrace.

Eventually they got up and showered but, as they dressed, Elena asked her boss-turned-lover what had brought about the change.

Declan had just pulled an Aran sweater over his head, a sweater she found particularly attractive. It was all she could do not to jump him again.

'You know how some men believe fellatio isn't the same thing as sex? I was trying to be one of those guys. I was thinking, well, it's OK if El goes down on me every day. I know she's my employee and all but it's not like we're having intercourse. I didn't expect this to happen but I've fallen in love with you. I want you to be my partner, not my factotum. I think we could be good together, El. I think we *are* good together.'

As Elena winkled into her jeans, she said, 'Well, partner. I was going to save this bit of news for later, but I'll go ahead and tell you now. I read that writing magazine you gave me and managed to sell an article to one of those glossy women's magazines. It's maudlin, nothing like the highbrow writing you do, but soon I'll be in the chips. Bet you didn't think I was such a quick study. I'm looking forward to taking *you* out to dinner when I get my cheque.'

Declan was strangely silent as he took in this news.

They continued getting dressed but Dec's face was now a mask of resignation.

'What's the matter, Dec? Aren't you happy for me? For us?'

'You don't need me anymore,' he said quietly.

She twined her arms round his neck and kissed him. Then she unzipped his trousers because they weren't going out anytime soon. Her palate was still craving the full measure of her lover's cock. Compared to his exquisite maleness, all other sustenance was beyond the pale.

'Oh, I need you, Declan. I haven't even begun to show you how much.'

She removed her clothes again and gestured for Dec to sit on the edge of the bed. Once she took his cock into her mouth, she felt a surge of energy that made her feel like the most desirable woman in the world. Yes, she needed this man. She needed him very much.

And, in her own way, she would make herself indispensable to the boss.

Welcome to Your New Job
Valerie Grey

The party had been going on for little more than an hour. I wore a nice black skirt and a white blouse that made me look rather plain. I stood in the corner of the ballroom sipping expensive champagne. I'd just started with the law firm as a paralegal a couple of months earlier. I didn't know anybody really and I didn't want to show up to the party at all but Tom, the attorney I worked for, insisted I come. I didn't want to say no; or rather I couldn't.

I saw one of the senior partners strolling across the ballroom floor, coming my way, and wanted to run to the ladies' room. His name was John Wheeler and he scared me, I don't know why exactly. I had no idea why he would come talk to me; I was a nobody, a new, simple paralegal, while he was the old hotshot lawyer. He was a god in the office; I didn't know the details of the case, but I'd heard he'd pulled a major coup the previous year, some class action that he'd manipulated brilliantly. He'd made a ton of money for the firm, and himself. Since then, he could do whatever he wanted in the firm and I'd heard he'd 'conquered' a number of the women in the office. Rumour had it he preferred anal sex and fucked them hard and left them quickly with broken hearts and pained asses. I had an aching in the pit of my stomach as he got closer. Maybe it was his eyes, the way he stared through me, like he was picking at my soul and determining what made me tick.

John stood right in front of me, almost engulfing me with his frame and blocking me from the rest of the guests at the party. The blood was pounding in my ears and my stomach was on fire.

He said, 'I've been watching you.'

My mouth was dry; I wanted to respond but I couldn't say anything. He had me pinned against the wall; I could feel his thick leg against mine holding me there.

'What are you doing?' I asked nervously.

He said, 'It's time.'

'Time, time for what?' I tried to stay calm but I could hear my voice cracking. I am petite, five foot four, and he was six foot three; I felt like a small animal trapped by a predatory beast.

He said, 'It's time for you to become my slave, of course.'

'What the hell are you talking about?' I tried to push him away, putting my hand on his rock-hard chest, but he didn't budge. He grabbed my wrist and twisted it. The pain made me tingle between the legs.

He said, 'I *know* you're a slut. I bet you want me to fuck you right now. You want my nine-inch cock up that little pussy, splitting you open.' He twisted my wrist even harder. I could feel the strain in my bones. 'You want me to make you scream right here? No one will care, believe me.'

I could feel the moulding on the wall pressing into my hips. I couldn't even see around him, he was so much bigger than I was.

I gave in. 'What ... what do you want?'

'I want you to go into the ladies' room and remove your panties. Don't say a word to anybody. Then go get me a drink, a Long Island Iced Tea. Then I want you to come right back to me and put your panties in my jacket pocket, understand?'

I couldn't take my eyes off his. The hair on the back of my neck stood up and a chill ran down my spine and my pussy started to get wet. John let go of my wrist. I rubbed my arm where he'd twisted it. His thigh was still against mine, pinning me up against the wall.

He said, 'You have ten minutes. If you're not back by then, you'll be punishedlater.'

He moved out of the way just enough for me to get by. I could feel the perspiration on my forehead. I thought

110

everybody was watching me as I moved through the crowd. It felt like my face was on fire as I made my way to the ladies' room. My legs were unstable. I slipped into one of the stalls and locked the door shut. I sat down on the toilet seat trying to catch my breath.

I considered sneaking out the back way. What could he do to me? I'd just avoid him at the office, I'd ... but what if, what if he did something *at* the office, what if he told people things? I couldn't afford to lose my job and there was a look in his eyes that made me afraid he'd do something to truly hurt me.

My pussy was a traitor, burning so ...

Three minutes. I didn't have much time. My hands felt like they were wrapped in huge awkward gloves as I slowly lifted my skirt and eased my panties over my hips. I couldn't believe how wet my pussy was; juices were running down my thighs.

I knew my face must have been scarlet when I returned to the party. I had to concentrate on each step; my legs felt weary and weak. I could feel the eyes on me; they all knew I wasn't wearing panties.

He hadn't moved an inch. He didn't react when he saw me, but I knew he was watching my every move.

I went to the bar and ordered a Long Island Iced Tea. I brought it to him, doing exactly as I was told. My voice was mousy when I greeted him; I could barely whisper out the words: 'Your drink, Mr Wheeler.'

111

He grabbed me by the shoulders and pushed me against the wall again and said, 'From now on you will call me *Master*, nothing else.'

I couldn't do anything; there was no place I could go and nothing I could do to get away.

'Do you have something for me?'

My hand shook so badly, I could barely grab my panties from my bag. I pulled them out and tried to hide them from view as I pushed them into his hand ... but he wouldn't take them.

'Sniff them for me, tell me what you smell.'

'Please,' I whispered, 'this has gone far enough.'

I felt his knee raise and press against my pussy. He started lifting me off the ground, spreading my legs as he forced me up. I tried to push down his leg but he was much too powerful for me.

'OK, OK, I'll smell them.'

I balled my panties in my hand and held them to my nose. I sniffed quickly and tried to put my hand down. John grabbed my wrist and pushed the sopping underwear back into my face.

'Tell me what you smell, slut.'

I could smell the musky scent of my sex; never before had it been this intense, this powerful. I knew anybody close by must have been able to smell it too.

John pulled my panties from my nose and put them in his pocket.

He said, 'Good girl.'

He eased his knee down so it wasn't up between my legs anymore. I could feel the heat of his chest. He grabbed my forearm and squeezed my wrist again.

'Let's get away from the crowd, slut.'

He literally dragged me through the mass of bodies in the ballroom and pushed me towards the elevator door.

'Get in!'

He shoved me in the empty car. I could see my reflection in the door of the mirrored compartment.

The elevator started to rise.

'You ... can't do this ... to me.' My voice was trembling; I could barely speak.

His cold blue eyes fixed on me but he didn't respond; he didn't need to. His eyes said: I can do whatever the fuck I want with you, slut.

The elevator door opened and he pushed me out into the hall, then grabbed my elbow so I wouldn't run. His large hand encircled my arm as he dragged me towards the open atrium that rose from the ballroom below. The music wafted up and echoed off the glass roof.

'Grab the railing and spread your legs.'

I looked over the edge. I could see the people mingling below, laughing and smiling, having a good time.

I felt John lift my skirt. I twisted my head and observed him pull a hard cock from his pants. Yes, he was at least nine inches but to me it seemed bigger. There was no way I could take a cock like that ...

I opened my dry mouth.

'Go ahead, scream.'

He took hold of my hips and pulled me back to him. I had to bite my lip in order to keep from screaming as the bulbous head of his cock pressed against my opening. My ears were ringing so loudly I could no longer hear the sounds of the party below. I closed my eyes and wept as his huge dick roughly penetrated me. My hands locked on the wooden railing and John slammed into me. With each violent thrust I was driven forwards till my upper body was pushed over the rail. I could see all the people gathered below. I was forced over the edge. My face was on fire and I prayed that nobody would look up and see me.

John had his hands on my hips and drove me forwards with his hips, pounding me and then pulling me back. I was a piece of meat to him, the new girl to use.

He grabbed my long black hair and twisted my head so I was looking at him. A jolt of electricity raced through my body as my eyes met his. The sound of his skin slapping against mine rang through my ears.

'I'm going to come in your cunt, you slut!'

Tears streamed down my cheeks as John pulled me back hard on his prick. I was jerked up off the ground. My knuckles were white from holding the rail so tightly, and my legs felt like they'd collapse. John's dick went in deep, filling me, hurting me with a good pain I dared not let him know about. The slap of his flesh against mine echoed in my mind. I bit my lip hard as I felt his dick start to twitch in my pussy. John slammed forwards, driving my hips against the rail; my torso was over the edge as his cock shot come into me. There was so much, it began to flow out as he continued to thrust and shoot.

When he finally pulled his dick free from my pussy it felt like there was a huge void in my belly. He grabbed my hair again and twisted me around, pressed on my shoulders and made me fall to my knees.

'Clean my cock!' he ordered.

His cock was right there, inches from my face. The slap across my face was sudden and unexpected. I could feel the burning of my cheek.

'Suck my cock clean, slut!'

I opened my mouth and the bulbous head of his dick made its way between my lips. There was no gentleness in his movements and he drove forwards, making me try to swallow him whole. I started to gag. I tried to pull my head off his dick but he held me firm. I was afraid I might vomit and knew that would probably turn him on … and me.

'Relax and suck me clean!'

I gagged on the slimy shaft; I couldn't get enough air and I could hear myself retching as my throat convulsed.

He pulled back on his cock ever so slightly and twisted my hair in his hand so hard that my scalp burned.

'*I said clean me!*'

I started working my tongue over the underside of his dick; I could feel the pulsing against my lips. I tried my best to suck the cock dry.

Just as I was allowing myself to enjoy this, John's hands left the back of my head and he slid his dick from my mouth.

'Zip me up, whore!'

John's cock was twitching inches in front of my face. My stomach was churning; I felt humiliated and ashamed. My hands trembled and I fumbled with his fly. I gently took his dick in my hand and eased it back into his pants, like a submarine mooring in a dock.

'Get up, slut.'

My legs were too weak. He pulled my up by my arms. I could feel his come seeping out of my pussy and, since I wasn't wearing panties, the man-juice began to roll down my thighs.

He grabbed an arm and pulled me towards the elevators. He said, 'You want to get home, don't you?' Those cold eyes were fixed on me but I couldn't react.

We descended into the ballroom, where the sound of the party hit me like a cruel slap as I stepped out of the elevator. John led me out the front door. I couldn't look anybody in the eyes; I knew they all must have seen me on the balcony getting fucked.

The valet brought John's car immediately. My ears were still ringing and I could feel the come dribbling out of my pussy as the young valet opened the door of the car for me.

My heart was beating like mad as John got in and put the car into gear. He told me: 'Do *not* touch yourself at all during the weekend. You're my slave now and you will do as I command.' His hand clamped on my thigh and squeezed. 'You no longer have any rights over your body and you will do what I say without question. You will come to my office at seven on Monday morning. I want you kneeling in front of my desk when I get there, with your hands up behind your head and your knees spread wide.'

I winced; he squeezed my flesh tighter.

'You are not to wear panties and I want you shaved smooth.'

The city streets were empty; he drove fast, recklessly.

'There will be more for you to learn later, but do you understand what I expect of you?'

I let out a cry of pain when John smacked me across the face.

'Do you understand?'

My mouth was so dry I could barely speak. 'Y-y-yes.' I couldn't look him in the eyes.

'Good.'

John's hand went up under my skirt. I grabbed the

door handle as his finger moved to my clit. I couldn't help feeling some pleasure as he rubbed gently.

His voice was serious and stern: 'You are not to touch yourself *at all*. You no longer have *the right* to reach orgasm without my permission ... slut, *do* you understand?'

I closed my legs on his hand as my body responded to his machinations. I slid back in the seat with the smooth, cool leather against my skin. I expected pleasure but I should have known better. John pinched my clit painfully between his fingers; his short manicured nails dug into my sensitive area and he twisted violently, making me almost scream.

'I said: *do you understand, slut*?'

'Yes, yes ...'

He moved his hand out from under my skirt. My nipples were hard and my chest was heaving. John reached across me and opened the door.

'Get out. You have the weekend. Be in my office seven sharp, otherwise you'll be punished beyond belief.'

John put his hands on the wheel and looked straight ahead, waiting for me to go. He looked so cold and cruel. I timidly got out of the car. He peeled away, leaving me alone in the dark blustery night, three blocks from my apartment building. My mind was a wreck; my heart was pounding in my chest and I could feel the perspiration covering my body.

I barely got more than a few hours of sleep on Saturday and Sunday. My mind was racing; I couldn't believe what had happened to me. Why had I let myself be treated that way? Why did it turn me on when it happened and why did I get wet when I recalled what John did to me? I thought about quitting the law firm, simply not showing up on Monday; but I had bills and rent and could not afford to spend weeks looking for new employment. And what if John or Human Resources did not give me a recommendation? I could always leave after a short stint there, I supposed. I didn't know what I was going to do.

Going to work Monday morning, I could feel the cool air on my pussy; it felt uncomfortable and wrong not having any panties on.

I arrived at 7a.m. sharp, as told. The receptionist wasn't in yet; I was happy at least she wouldn't see me like this. Half the lights weren't even on as I headed slowly towards John's office. With each step I could feel my chest tighten, and my head started pounding. My hand quivered when I knocked on John's door; it was ajar and I could see a light on inside.

The sound of my knuckles rapping on the smooth, hard mahogany echoed in my ears like the trumpets of angels calling forth Armageddon.

There was no answer. I gently pushed open the door and stepped inside, taking small steps.

The office was large and dark but there was a small

light on at the desk. The walls were covered with shelves and shelves of books, law books, fiction books, even some volumes of Victorian erotica.

I wasn't alone. I saw John's secretary kneeling on the floor in front of his desk. She didn't move; she didn't turn to look at me. I'd seen Marilyn around the office but we'd never spoken. She was a beautiful Chinese girl, not much taller than me, late twenties, very thin with tiny breasts and gorgeous long black hair. She wore a dark suit with a jacket and short skirt, and black-rimmed glasses. She looked more like a smart lawyer ready for court, not an assistant dominated by her boss.

I yelped as a hand fell on my shoulder. John loomed behind me like the Devil over the damned.

'I *told* you to kneel in front of my desk with your knees wide.'

I was shocked when he slapped my face with an open hand; it happened so quickly, I was not prepared for the treatment.

'*Get into position, slut!*'

John pushed me forwards and I was next to Marilyn. I didn't have any choice but to fall to my knees beside her. I saw that she had a dildo in her mouth; it was huge, and a good three inches jutted from her widely spread lips. I could see the small bulge in the back of her throat where the head of the rubber cock came to a rest.

'Hands behind your head, slut!'

I felt fear in the pit of my stomach, yet my pussy was wet now. I put my hands behind my head and intertwined my fingers. John casually started spreading papers out on his desk.

I could feel the strain in my thighs already from kneeling, and keeping my legs so wide.

'You're dismissed, cunt,' John said; he didn't look up as Marilyn got to her feet.

She pulled the long dildo from between her teeth and placed it into her suit-jacket pocket. She said, 'Thank you, Master.'

'Close the door on your way out, cunt.'

I felt Marilyn shuffle past me. My arms shuddered when the door slammed shut, leaving me alone with John.

Part of me wanted desperately to beg for freedom, but I didn't know what to say that would convince him; the other part wanted him to toss me on that desk and fuck me like he had Friday night: roughly, assuredly, making me his meat.

John continued to look at *The Wall Street Journal* as he spoke: 'You will be punished later, slut. I expect when *I tell* you to *do* something, that you *do it*, there are *no* fucking excuses.'

John moved from behind his huge desk. My thighs burned and my knees shook. He had his cock out of his trousers and stood before me. The head of his member was two inches away from my lips and I could smell the cologne he had on, strong and masculine, mixed with the mustiness of his crotch.

'Open up, slut!'

Again I was surprised by the sudden slap across my face; and surprised how my pussy reacted with heat and moisture.

'Suck my cock, slut!'

I reached for his cock but John grabbed my wrists, squeezed them tight and lifted my hands up above my head.

'Only use your *mouth*, slut, *no hands*.'

John thrust his hips forwards and forced his dick between my lips. I started to gag as he forced the head of his cock to the back of my throat. He held my hands tight in and pulled me towards him, driving his prick ever deeper. I thought I might puke all over him. What would he do if that happened?

'Do it, slut, *make me come*!'

I coughed and choked as John's thick member filled me. Tears streaked my cheeks as he fucked my face. Gobs of saliva leaked out of my mouth and dripped to the floor.

'Come on, slut, *do* something!'

I felt him squeeze my wrists tighter. I tried desperately; again and again my mouth slid over the length of John's shaft. My jaws were aching and I'd never felt so ashamed and aroused simultaneously.

'You better swallow all my come, slut. You wouldn't want it dripping on your suit.'

My jaw was spread wide. The thought of his come on my jacket had never occurred to me – everybody would know with that evidence – and then he started to come. The thick spunk filled my mouth. It seemed like it would never stop. I tried to pull myself off his dick, but John held me firm as he kept pumping his come and my puke into my mouth. My throat involuntarily convulsed on his cock as I desperately tried to swallow the copious load.

John pulled his prick free from my lips and let go of my hands. There was nothing I could do but swallow the come that filled my mouth.

'Marilyn, come here, please.'

John spoke into the monitor on his desk. Marilyn rushed inside, fell to her knees and took his cock in her mouth without a word. He cupped the back of her head and she licked him clean.

'Thank you, cunt.'

Marilyn gently eased John's prick back into his pants and zipped him up. She remained on her knees, head down as he ran his finger through her long black hair.

'You may go to your desk, my cunt.'

Marilyn got to her feet and disappeared out the door in an instant.

I could still taste the thick come and puke in my mouth. I wanted desperately to spit it out, to have a martini or something to get rid of the awful taste.

I stayed on my knees and softly sobbed.

A sharp, harsh commanding flavour to John's voice: 'I told you I want *your hands* behind *your head*!'

John smacked his open hand down on the desk. I could feel his eyes on me but I didn't dare look up. I lifted my trembling arms behind my head and wound my fingers together.

'You need to work on your cocksucking skills, slut. You've got to make me come, *that's* your job. I don't just want some lifeless gloryhole to stick my dick in.'

No one had ever spoken to me like that before; I was appalled and turned on by his words.

John moved around in front of the desk. 'This is for you, a gift.'

He set a huge purple dildo on the floor; it was just like the one Marilyn had had in her mouth. It was probably twelve inches long, thick and ribbed.

'Welcome to our law offices,' he said.

And I replied, 'Thank you, Master.'

Keeping It Real
Giselle Renarde

She burst into his home office without knocking. Favourite clients needn't bother with formalities – especially not favourite clients who'd just been named World's Sexiest Woman by *Spotlite* magazine.

'Marcel, did you see?'Peradice held up the magazine like an old-school newsie. 'Extra, extra! Read all about it: girl from the projects rises to rap super-stardom, wins world's love!'

Marcel was on the telephone, and he held his finger to his lips, then pointed to one of the plush chairs. Her manager's home office was much more comfy than the one downtown. Even so, she liked the tower better. Here, she was always afraid his wife would walk in on them. Marcel claimed he told Dalena everything, but guys always said that.

'Did you see?' she asked again when he'd hung up the

phone. Peradice showcased the magazine enthusiastically, like those bimbos on *The Price Is Right*. 'Get a load of my tits in that halter top! Even I want to fuck me.'

Marcel's chair squeaked as he leaned back, arching his hands, tapping his fingertips together. He didn't look too happy, and Peradice couldn't understand why. This was the greatest news since she'd won Best Album of the Year.

'What's wrong?' she asked, setting the magazine on his desk. She really wanted him to look at it.

When he did, he shrugged and said, 'They airbrushed the hell out of you.'

Peradice didn't know how to feel. Her heart turned icy, but her belly was on fire. 'So what? They airbrush everyone.'

Where was he going with this?

Marcel creaked back in his chair, tossed his feet on his desk, crossed them at the ankles. 'You're getting a little full of yourself, Per.'

That hurt, but Peradice didn't get where she was today by letting people see her true feelings. Not even Marcel, and she trusted him better than anyone. She sucked her teeth. 'I got every reason to be full of myself. I ain't no little white boy growing up in the suburbs with mommy and daddy paying my way. You know how I got to where I am?'

'Yes, Per.'

'I worked my ass off is how, fighting for studio sessions

with dicks who're grabbing at me the whole time. I could have lived my whole life in the projects muttering about how the man was keeping me down, but no. Instead I rap about it. I make people listen, and when they hear my truth it changes them. Don't you tell me I don't deserve respect. I built this empire.'

'Yes, I heard your Grammy speech, but thanks for the recap.' Marcel stared at her with this amused little smirk on his face that made her feel nakedly transparent. 'Are you waiting for a standing ovation?'

Peradice decided to ignore his little game and get what she'd really come for. 'How about a plain old standing O?' Leaning against his desk, she popped her hips to draw attention to her luscious ass. 'You want me?'

He looked, that was for damn sure, and Peradice felt confident he wouldn't be able to pass up a quickie. But he didn't move. He looked, but didn't touch.

'What's your problem, Marcel?' She crossed her arms in front of her chest, drawing attention to her cleavage. 'You got the world's sexiest woman right in front of you and you act like you're not interested.'

'I'm interested in *you*,' he said. 'But check your attitude at the door.'

She forced laughter, though the sentiment hit close to home. 'You sound like my mother.'

'Well, you're paying for my advice, so you might as well take it.' He was getting stern now, which always turned her on more than his kindness. And he *was* a kind man. She knew he really cared.

'Where do you get off thinking you're better than everybody?' he asked.

'I don't think that!'

'Don't you?'

Sometimes Marcel brought out Peradice's inner brat. 'Maybe I *am* better than you. I wouldn't be stupid enough to pass up a sure thing.'

Marcel stood up behind his desk, mirroring her stance, arms crossed before his chest. His expression was stone. It made her quiver. Was he angry? Had she really pissed him off this time?

'Who's the boss around here, Peradice?'

She raised an eyebrow. 'Tony Danza.'

'Be serious for two seconds.' He wasn't moving, not twitching, not scratching, and that made Peradice seriously uneasy. Was this the calm before the storm?

Something in the strength of his gaze told her to sit, and she followed that silent instruction, feeling vulnerable and fascinated. 'You're the boss.'

'Am I?' Marcel cocked his head, and a look came over him she might have mistaken for pity. 'Then why don't you listen? Why don't you take my advice?'

Now she felt a little lost. 'Marcel, baby, I don't know what I did. What advice?'

'Don't let it go to your head,' he clarified. 'I told you

that right from the beginning. God, I want to spank some sense into you.'

Something perked inside of her and she cried out, 'OK.'

For a moment, he said nothing. His gaze darkened, which she'd seen often enough, but something was different today. This wasn't play. He wasn't teasing.

That was OK, because neither was she.

'You're right,' Peradice agreed, feeling much more herself than she had in past months. She'd spent too much time posing in designer threads. 'If I get all caught up in my success, I move away from my roots, and my roots are what got me here. I gotta stay true to them, and to you. I mean, without you I'd be lost. A girl from the projects can't navigate the music industry on her own, not without getting royally screwed.'

Finally a smile broke across Marcel's lips. 'I thought you liked getting screwed.'

His voice was gravel, and that deep textured resonance brought a thick pulse between Peradice's legs. She went to him, clawed at his shirt, tugged at the buttons. 'Baby, I want you so bad. I dream of you every night. I can't get you out of my mind.'

Marcel held up one hand to stop her from talking. God, he was sexy when he took charge.

'Back to basics,' he commanded. 'You were young and naïve when you came to me. You're more sophisticated now, but your popularity's got you thinking you're invincible. I need you to put yourself back in my hands. I need you to trust me.'

'I do trust you,' she said, shocked that he'd think otherwise.

'Will you do what I say?'

That was difficult. 'I don't know, Marcel. I'm not gonna write you a blank cheque. You gotta tell me what you want first.'

'I will tell you,' he agreed, his expression calm but still brutally firm. 'And, as I dole out instructions, you'll acknowledge and obey. Understood?'

'Yes, boss.' Peradice loved it when he acted this way, domineering and father-knows-best. She had such high regard for him, utter and complete faith in his knowledge and abilities. 'Whatever you say.'

'Good.' He actually smiled, but it was the kind that put her even more on edge. She'd rather stick with the glare. It didn't make her quite so anxious. 'Now take off your clothes.'

A giddy thrill ran through her, and she peeled off her cotton T-shirt and tossed it on the floor.

'Pick that up,' Marcel instructed. 'Don't throw clothes all over the place. Fold it and place it on that chair.'

She did as he asked, even if the request sounded a little dumb. So much for living in the moment, taking the bull by the horns. She slid her jeans down, then folded them with her top. Barefoot, she kicked off her panties, unhooked her bra and placed everything on the chair.

Then she remembered the door.

'Oh shit,' she said, racing for it.

'Hold up!' It wasn't often Marcel used that tone with her, and her pussy clenched in response. 'Stop right there. Turn around.'

She did, but explained, 'I didn't lock the door.'

'Leave it,' he instructed, shifting out of his white shirt and hanging it over the back of his chair.

'But what if someone comes in while we're –'

'Don't you worry about it.' Marcel grinned, but it wasn't his face she was interested in. God, that chest. Peradice always wondered where he found time to hit the gym. Those weren't the abs of a workaholic.

'Kneel on the rug.' Marcel was rarely domineering, so Peradice followed his instructions cautiously, but she couldn't deny her arousal. Her clit ached so badly she started rubbing it against the back of her foot. Ooh, that felt good.

'Why are you hiding behind your desk?' she asked provocatively. She knew exactly how to turn him on. At least, she thought she did. 'Why don't you come over here and shove your cock in my mouth?'

'Why don't you quiet down and let someone else do the talking for once?' His tone was measured and strong, but the words shocked her.

Peradice's spine straightened, and she furrowed her brow deliberately. Her breasts stuck out when she held this position, her nipples so cold from the conditioned air that they strained forwards. 'Nobody puts me in my place, Marcel. Not even you.'

'Of course not,' Marcel said, with gravel in his voice. 'You're Queen of the World, sexiest woman, superior to all others. Peradice knows best.'

'I never said I was better than anybody,' she shot back, though maybe she'd implied it.

'Sure you did.' Marcel picked up her magazine, walked around his desk and sat on her clothes to flip through it. 'I won't deny that you're gorgeous, honey, but once the fame goes to your head you're a goner. Let's circumvent that fate.'

'What are you talking about?' she asked, as he reached for his phone. None of this was making sense.

'Dalena, she's here,' Marcel said into the receiver. 'And she's naked.'

Peradice gasped, sprang up from the rug and tried to dig her clothes out from under Marcel. 'What are you doing? You told your wife about us?'

Marcel didn't budge. Her clothes remained buried under his butt. 'Of course,' he scoffed. 'I told you I don't keep secrets from Dalena.'

'Yeah, but I didn't believe you.'

His expression hardened, which was frightening

because it had been hard enough to begin with. 'I also told you to kneel on the rug. Get down.'

'I'm not a dog,' Peradice shot back, racing behind his desk for the one item of clothing still out in the open. She threw his white shirt over her shoulders just as his office door opened.

Peradice's heart plunged into her feet when Dalena walked in wearing a short kimono. Not many women could pull off orange silk, but that colour played off the tint of Dalena's kinky hair. This wasn't the first time they'd met, but everything seemed different now.

Once Dalena had closed the door, she untied her belt and let her kimono slip from her shoulders. 'Good to see you, Peradice. Congratulations on your new title.'

'Quit hiding behind that chair,' Marcel instructed, waving Peradice over.

'Should I hide under your desk instead?'

'I don't want you hiding anywhere,' Marcel answered. 'Come out and kneel on the rug.'

Peradice's heart raced, because 'on the rug' was exactly where Dalena stood. Naked.

'You said you'd follow my instructions,' Marcel reminded her. 'This is only an exercise, Per. Cooperating takes nothing away from you.'

'Yes, love,' Dalena added. 'Do as you're told. Have faith in my husband.'

Peradice's mind raced as she looked back and forth

between husband and wife. She couldn't seem to settle on one emotion. She felt sheepish and guilty for sleeping with this woman's husband, but also jealous of the way Marcel was ogling his wife right in front of her. On top of all that, she was more than a little afraid of what this pair was up to.

She couldn't bring herself to look at Dalena, and instead asked Marcel, 'What's going on?'

Without so much as glancing away from his wife, Marcel pointed to the rug. 'Kneel.'

'But why?' Peradice whined. 'Tell me what's happening.'

'Kneel.'

And then Dalena said it too. 'Kneel.'

Confounded, Peradice stumbled to the rug. Dalena stood with her heels up against the couch, her back to the solarium window. Hopefully the gardener had today off. God only knows what he'd tell the press.

Peradice sank to her knees, facing Marcel, but he instructed her to turn around. When she did, her face was pretty much right up against his wife's pussy. Peradice had to lean back to keep her lips from touching Dalena's trim pubic hair, but there was nothing she could do to prevent the aroma of hot cunt from infiltrating her nostrils. As much as she resisted, her pussy pulsed conspiratorially.

'Do you know how many people exist on this planet?' Marcel asked. 'Peradice?'

'Oh.' Did she? The information was probably in there somewhere, but right now she was too taken with the coconut scent of his wife's skin to think. 'No, I don't.'

'Seven billion,' Dalena answered. 'A little more than half the world's population is female.'

'Wow,' Peradice said, feeling her hot breath recoil off Dalena's skin. She closed her eyes, and her heart thudded so loudly she was certain they could both hear it.

'Over three and a half billion women in the world,' Marcel went on. She could hear him rising from that chair where she'd folded all her clothes. Ominously, he walked towards her. She could feel him looming behind her back. 'Do you really think you're the sexiest? In the whole world?'

How could she answer a question like that? It made her feel argumentative that he would even ask. 'I never said I was the world's sexiest woman, it was *Spotlite* magazine that said so.'

'Look at my wife,' Marcel instructed. 'Tilt your head and get a good look.'

Peradice felt strange ogling Marcel's wife, but she did as requested and followed the sweet curve of Dalena's thighs up past her ample hips and milky-brown belly. Bashfully, she met the woman's dark eyes, and when Dalena offered a dimpled smile she was in heaven.

'What about my wife?' Marcel probed. 'Don't you think she's sexy?'

'Yes.' The word was like chocolate on Peradice's tongue. 'Very sexy.'

'Thank you,' Dalena said, blushing a tad. 'I'm glad you think so, because I want you to lick my pussy.'

Peradice was never shocked when guys came on to her, but this was new. There was a pervasive anti-gay sentiment in her community, and that was probably the biggest reason she'd never acted on her throbbing impulses. In truth, Peradice was just as attracted to women as she was to men.

'But first I want you to button up that shirt,' Marcel said.

She started to shrug it off, then processed his words and glanced back at him, puzzled. 'Button it up?'

'Yes,' he said firmly.

His shirt was miles too big for her, and it seemed odd that he wanted her body covered rather than exposed, but she did as he asked. When she'd done it up almost right to the top, Marcel grabbed the too-long shirtsleeves and pulled them around her body so her arms criss-crossed her breasts. Pulling tight, he tied the sleeves behind her back and she was stuck like that, nearly immobile.

'It's time.' His hand was heavy on her head, tilting it back. 'Lick my wife's pussy.'

Peradice chuckled nervously. 'I don't really know how.'

'Lick it like a cat with cream,' Dalena said encouragingly. 'Be gentle at first.'

Marcel stood directly behind Peradice, lifting her towards Dalena's pussy, his crotch blazing. She felt a little claustrophobic, sandwiched between them like this. When she leaned back, her shoulders met Marcel's thighs. There was no escape.

'Lick it,' Marcel encouraged.

Dalena spread her pussy lips with her fingers, revealing the glistening pink inside. 'Lick it, my beauty.'

'OK,' Peradice agreed.

She felt like she was in a dream the moment her tongue lolled out of her mouth. Dalena's clit was close, housed by pink folds of flesh, and Peradice couldn't resist. Inching forwards, she followed the luscious aroma of hot pussy until the tip of her tongue was nudging Dalena's clit, up and down, barely budging.

'Oh yes,' Dalena cried, arching forwards and spreading her legs. Peradice had hardly done anything, and already the woman was halfway to ecstasy. 'Use your whole tongue.'

Peradice followed the instruction, flattening her tongue against Dalena's hot pussy and lapping those gorgeous wet lips. There was something oddly familiar about the taste of this woman's cunt: tangy, musty, rich. It planted its aroma at the roof of Peradice's mouth and clung to her throat when she swallowed.

'Stick to my clit, sexy.' Dalena held the sides of her head now, keeping her in the optimal position. Marcel's wife sure knew what she liked, and she wasn't afraid of crying out when Peradice licked that perfect place. 'Oh yes, you got it, right there.'

Peradice couldn't move. All she was capable of in that moment was licking Dalena's clit relentlessly, so hard and fast her jaw started to hurt. She couldn't keep up with the amount of juice Dalena's pussy was spilling across her lips, and it soaked her chin and dripped down her exposed cleavage. Closing her eyes, Peradice pictured Dalena's nectar soaking into Marcel's white shirt, and the image made her feel both aroused and unsettled.

This woman knew Peradice was sleeping with her husband, and what? Didn't care? If it were Peradice, she'd be slapping her man's mistress upside the head, not feeding the girl pussy. She didn't understand Dalena, but she had to admit she was grateful ... and so turned on that juice drenched her thighs.

Marcel grabbed Peradice's shoulders and pulled her against him. The man's cock was so hard beneath his trousers that his erection pummelled her neck as Dalena closed the gap. The world seemed a little darker between two bodies, and it was getting hard to breathe. The tangy scent of pussy was everywhere, all over her face, filling her nostrils, making her dizzy as Dalena rubbed that sweet clit against her tongue.

'Oh yes, you sexy little bitch.' Writhing roughly, wildly, Dalena scoured herself against Peradice's face. 'Lick my pussy. Lick it hard, harder!'

Dalena's body seemed to be everywhere at once, suffocating Peradice with every shimmy and thrust. She struggled impotently, forwards against Dalena and then back against Marcel, but she wasn't going anywhere in her makeshift straightjacket. All she could hope to do was eat her way out, and she worked at Dalena's clit so voraciously the woman shouted accolades. 'Oh yes, baby. Lick it! Fuck, you're gonna make me come. I'm gonna come, I'm gonna come!'

Peradice ate harder, despite the soreness in her jaw, despite her lack of breath. She licked and lapped as Dalena hovered on the edge of orgasm, then finally sent the woman over by drawing that fat clit between her lips and sucking it like a cock.

'Oh fuck!' Dalena screamed, crashing her pussy into Peradice's face, plunging into her orgasm like an ocean diver. 'You get me off so goooooood!'

Dalena fucked her face until Peradice lost her tenuous hold on that engorged clit. It popped out from between her lips, but Dalena didn't stop there. Peradice opened her mouth and the woman went on grinding against her tongue.

Just when Peradice thought this moment of supreme ecstasy would never end, Dalena released a tortured shriek and fell back on the couch. 'Oh, God, I can't stand another second of it. You've licked me raw, little girl.'

Peradice didn't appreciate being called a little girl, but she was too stunned and dizzied to object. She stared straight ahead, into Dalena's hot cunt, its lips spread like glistening red flower petals. There was some satisfaction in knowing her tongue had created that arousal.

'I think I've waited long enough,' Marcel chimed in, jerking Peradice to her feet. 'My turn now.'

Her heart jumped when she heard him unzip his fly, and she wanted to look at Dalena, judge his wife's reaction, but she felt too weirdly ashamed to even glance in the woman's direction.

'Spread your legs,' Marcel instructed, and she did, but it wasn't easy to move with her hands tied up. 'A little wider.'

When she'd positioned herself well enough to suit his needs, Marcel took firm hold of her shoulders and bent her over so fast all the blood rushed to her brain. She was swimming, not knowing where she'd stop until her cheek landed against Dalena's warm breast.

'Lick them while he fucks you,' the beautiful wife instructed.

Peradice tried to lift her head, but it was impossible without leverage. 'I can't.'

Marcel tossed her shirttails up over her bare ass and smacked it. Hard. 'You do as my wife commands,' he said before bringing his sizzling cockhead to her slit. 'Or you don't get fucked.'

Oh, God, she wanted him inside her! She would do anything to feel his thick length streaming through her pussy, just burying itself in her wetness and ramming her again and again. She needed it. Now.

'Please,' she whimpered. 'Please fuck me.'

'Only if you suck my tits,' Dalena taunted, pushing her breasts together under Peradice's cheek.

Marcel's cockhead sat at the entrance to her pussy like hot, throbbing steel enrobed in silk. She tried to buck back and steal a fuck, but it was just too hard to move. Her head felt like a bowling ball against the pillow of Dalena's breast and she struggled to raise it, just a little, just enough to get her mouth to the nearest nipple.

Dalena gasped when Peradice licked it. 'Yes! Oh yes, that's very good.'

Marcel must have been watching over her shoulder, because he applauded her movement too, and awarded her with his cock. Her body jumped as he entered far more swiftly than she'd anticipated. In this position, standing hunched over Dalena, arms bound straightjacket style, she could do nothing to temper his thrusts. His cockhead throbbed inside her, banging against her outer edges.

Peradice tightened her pussy muscles to hinder his rapid movement, and it worked to a certain extent. Marcel groaned as she milked his erection, and his enjoyment only goaded her further. So did Dalena's. When the luscious woman groaned hungrily, Peradice licked her nipple, then sucked it, then licked and sucked in turn.

As Marcel dug his fingers into her hips and thrust

ferociously, Peradice found herself sucking Dalena's poor tit harder than she should have. Her manager's lovely wife started to hiss and whine, then pushed up on Peradice's shoulders with obvious effort, setting her mouth down on the other nipple. Peradice took to it like a suckling babe, eager and hungry.

'Fuck, I'm not gonna last long in this tight little cunt,' Marcel said.

'Her tongue feels so good on my tits,' Dalena said. 'God, she might make me come again just from this.'

It felt strange, being talked about like she wasn't in the room, but Peradice sort of liked it. She was always the focus of attention wherever she went. It felt good to be their toy. She wanted to make them happy, and she sucked Dalena's nipple generously while she milked Marcel's cock.

'Fuck, yeah.' Marcel gripped her hips, plunging deep inside her pussy. She tried to buck back, give him more, but it was just impossible. He didn't seem to care. He just kept shouting, 'God, your pussy's tight. You grip me so good.'

'She's so sexy,' Dalena added. Her voice was breathy and thin.

Peradice wished she could call Dalena sexy too, but she just couldn't raise her head away from that erect nipple. Marcel rammed her from behind, knocking her forwards every time his pelvis whacked her ass, but Dalena caught her shoulders, steadying her. She was safe in their hands.

'Fuck, this is it!' Marcel grunted as he shoved his thick cock into her. He held there, his erection throbbing like a heartbeat in her pussy, and then released a reverberating growl. If she didn't know better, Peradice would have sworn she felt the heat of his come exploding from his cockhead and filling her cunt with white-hot warmth.

'Oh, baby,' Dalena cooed. 'You look so good like that.'

Peradice circled around that pebbled nipple, and shrieked when Marcel grabbed her shoulders and pulled her upright. His spent cock escaped her pussy, and right away she felt his cream drizzling down her thigh. She loved that.

Dalena gazed up from the couch, smiling. 'What a day! The world's sexiest woman ate my pussy.'

'And sucked your tits,' Marcel added, draping his arms around Peradice as he gently kissed her cheek. 'And learned a thing or two about humility, I bet.'

'I was humble already,' she countered, savouring Marcel's sweet embrace and the love in Dalena's eyes. 'But you're right – there are sexier women than me in the world. Hell, there's one right here.'

Smiling, Dalena blew her a kiss.

The Birthday Goddess
Dominic Santi

Among our closest group of friends, the one absolute requirement of each birthday celebration was that we act out the birthday person's hottest sexual fantasy. The eight of us – four men and four women – had known each other since college, and as couples had fucked around with each other long enough that we were comfortable with the sex between us being pretty much no-holds-barred. We were all bisexual, leaning towards hetero and married that way, though with no great inhibitions. We were into voyeurism and exhibitionism, and we loved seeking new sexual thrills. Most importantly, we knew each other's limits – and where there was ample room for pushing the envelope.

Everything else was just details. When the eight of us laid out the birthday-party ground rules, we decided every aspect of each celebration would be part of providing a feast of absolute sexual indulgence. For example, it would be OK for a woman to demand oral sex to orgasm from every person in the room, repeated until she'd passed out or at least screamed herself hoarse from coming. She would not, however, be required to reciprocate with a single blowjob or pussy licking – unless sucking cock or eating pussy was part of *her* fantasy. It was her birthday, and she not only got whatever cake she wanted, she got to eat it however she wished.

We all had good jobs, so we laughingly added that the birthday person's spouse would be required to provide a shopping spree in which they would spring for a new outfit and whatever other accoutrements the birthday person deemed necessary to make his or her fantasy come to life. My wife was a slave to fashion, so I groaned – though, at her raised eyebrow, I quickly voted 'yes' – when she added the caveat that the birthday person be entitled to be as greedy as he or she decided the spouse's finances could handle. Just as I expected: over the years my credit cards had handled a lot for her birthday fantasies. It was so fucking worth it!

Merlina's thirty-sixth birthday was Saturday, and I was already hard thinking about it. She had announced that her fantasy this year was to be a sex goddess. Until the stroke of midnight, she wanted absolute service and obedience. And she wanted every erogenous zone in her body licked, sucked and fucked to screaming orgasmic perfection – as many times as she could stand. She wanted to be *worshipped*!

I took her shopping after work on Tuesday. My face flamed with embarrassment when she tugged me into the private changing room of her favourite boutique, theoretically to get my opinion on whether the dress suited her. One look, and my cock knew it suited her fine. She turned from side to side, checking out her reflection in the mirror as she trailed her fingers down the low-cut front of a dress so short it was almost a waste of fabric. Almost. The white jersey knit clung to her like a second skin, hugging the curves of her firm round hips, teasing her nipples to long stiff points. She did a slow sexy pirouette, then held out her arms and stepped towards me with her eyebrows raised.

I took my time 'deciding', circling my palms over her nipples. My hands were big. Her breasts filled them perfectly, the all-natural fullness resting heavily against my palms. When my shorts were wet with pre-come and Merlina was breathing hard, she booted me out of the changing room and told me to give my credit card to the clerk, a very professional young lady who was obviously trying very hard not to grin. I blushed and my cock got even harder, knowing she knew what we'd been doing.

Merlina walked out of the dressing room and announced – to me as well as the clerk and the three professionally attired women carrying briefcases who'd just come in the front door – that she wanted lots of anticipation leading up to her birthday. So, from that moment on, no more sex until the big day.

'That's Saturday,' she said, smiling at the clerk. 'Five days from now. Do you think he'll last?'

I blushed again with embarrassment, which immediately had my cock spearing out into my trousers. As the women around us tittered, I leaned forwards, being careful to keep facing the counter, and whispered to Merlina that she hadn't warned me of my impending celibacy.

Merlina stepped back, turned me towards her and looked pointedly down at my crotch. Then she looked back up and loudly announced that servants didn't get to be part of the decision-making process. As I stared at her in shock, she added that I wasn't allowed to masturbate until Saturday, either.

She said exactly that, loudly and clearly: 'You're not to masturbate either.'

Though she then added, *sotto voce*, that, since today wasn't her birthday, she couldn't technically forbid me to do so – yet. However, she'd appreciate it if I refrained as she wished, so I'd be horny enough to worship her as she intended to be worshipped on her big day.

I was so embarrassed, and it turned me on so much, I almost came in my pants. And dammit, Merlina knew.

'I'll make it worth your while, love,' she purred, patting my startled bottom as she kissed my cheek. Then she turned and sashayed towards the door.

My face burning and my throbbing cock seeping, I swallowed hard and handed over my credit card. The sales clerk quickly rang up the dress, along with the pile of silky underthings Merlina had selected. The female lingerie was not all in Merlina's size, and the four matching male G-strings were clearly not all going to fit me. The sales girl glanced at my bulging crotch and held up a black silk pouch obviously designed for someone considerably more endowed than I. She smirked, and I came in my pants.

I had to walk with my jacket in front of me, but, when I shamefacedly explained why, Merlina grinned and announced that, despite my lack of control, we were still going to stop at the jewellers on the way home. I cringed when she picked out a small but elegant gold tiara edged with tiny, perfect pearls. But I dutifully handed over my credit card, not even caring that doing so made my cock twitch again. Apparently, one of the advantages of being a married goddess was knowing exactly how much a worshipful husband's bank account could handle without doing real damage to the family finances.

The moment we got home, she hung her dress on the closet door. 'Foreplay,' she told me, more times than I could count over the next few days. Every time, she ran her fingers over the shimmering material, then over her nipples. Every time, my erection and I watched helplessly from the other side of the room. The anticipation and the damn near constant hard-on were almost killing me. When I told her so, she grinned and pinched her nipple again–and blew me a kiss. If she hadn't forbidden me to come, I would have, right then. It was one of the hottest things she'd ever done.

By Saturday afternoon, I was calling it the blue-balls dress, because that was exactly what looking at the damn thing was giving me. Merlina had spent four hours at the salon, getting her hair and nails done and her whole body waxed in ways she assured me had her skin satiny smooth and humming, especially in all the places I didn't get to see – until tonight. When she walked out of the bathroom from her shower, she was wearing shimmering ivory silk hose and a lacy garter belt with tiny matching panties and bra.

My hands froze on my tie. At Merlina's instruction, I was wearing a tuxedo – part of what she'd decided was appropriate attire for worshipping a goddess. Instinctively, I started towards her, my cock jutting out into the little black pouch encasing it. Merlina held a finger up and shook her head.

'Not yet, sweetie,' she purred. 'I want you truly primed to service me.' She circled her palms over her nipples. They poked up hard and proud into the see-through white lace. 'I am so ready to be worshipped!'

My throat was too dry to speak. I shoved my hands in my pockets, watching Merlina fondle her tits while she shimmied into her awesome goddess dress and her strappy stiletto fuck-me heels. She placed her tiara on her perfectly styled hair, the pearls and gold shimmering in her glorious dark waves, and suddenly she really did look like a goddess. My goddess! I couldn't wait to service her. All I could think about was how it was only a couple more hours until I got to lick and suck and fuck her mouth and her tits and her cunt and her ass until she'd orgasmed so many times she couldn't walk any better than I could right now, which wasn't very well at all, because *fuck*, my balls ached!

And I was going to get to worship her in front of all my closest friends. Fuck, just the thought of how exposed and embarrassed I was going to be had my dick diamond-hard. The wicked glint in Merlina's eyes told me she knew exactly how much her fantasy was turning me on–and how wet she was getting watching me. God, I loved her for it!

By six o'clock, we were at our best friends' house. Kay and Jim had a large modern home at the edge of a small city a half-hour down the interstate. A huge family room with plush white carpet and floor-to-ceiling glass doors looked out on the garden and its eight-foot privacy fence. Kay had the windows open, letting in the breeze and the scent of honeysuckle and night-blooming jasmine.

For Merlina's fantasy evening, they'd replaced the regular furniture with three queen-sized mattresses made up with white satin sheets, piles of large fluffy pillows and a single reclining couch like the ones in movies about ancient Greeks. The couch was next to their formal dining table, which was pushed back against one wall and covered with a crisp white linen tablecloth. Atop the table were deep-blue goblets and small plates with gold rims, carafes of wine and water, and a spread of food that made my mouth water even before I got close enough to smell. There were bite-sized meats and vegetables and hard-boiled eggs, cheeses and bananas and grapes and huge strawberries by a pot of chocolate fondue.

'All finger food, as commanded by our goddess,' Kay said with a laugh, pointing out that there was not a single piece of silverware on the table. 'There are warm hand towels in the covered dish by the napkins, if anything really gets messy. Welcome to Merlina's temple!'

At Merlina's direction, we sampled appetisers and a single glass of wine each while we waited for Mike and Audrey and Stan and Elaine to arrive. When we were all together – the women in elegant, form-hugging white silk sheaths, the men in tuxedos that did nothing to hide our erections – we went over Merlina's wishes for the evening. I don't remember what I ate. All I could see was my beautiful wife in her golden tiara and that glorious fucking white dress.

At 6.30 on the dot, Kay took Merlina's hand and led her down the hall to the huge master bath with the spa-sized sunken ceramic tub that had been the focus of more than one birthday fantasy. Audrey and Elaine quickly followed. By Merlina's wish, the evening was starting with a candlelit re-enactment of the birth of Venus, beginning with Venus being bathed, at length and intimately, by all the women – and only the women – taking part in her birthday fantasy.

'You may have one more half-glass of wine each,' Merlina called over her shoulder. 'And strip to your slave belts. That's an order from your goddess. This first part's just for girls, but we'll call you to watch in a few minutes.'

I'd seen the other women in our group naked often enough to know that, even without this week's deprivation, I was going to be hard pressed not to come just watching them pleasuring each other's glistening bodies in thigh-deep, scented water. I decided right then and there that I wasn't going to be concerned if I shot on the bathroom floor. If watching my naked wife being worshipped by other naked women was more than I could handle, I was willing to admit my weakness.

As our pants fell to the floor at the edge of the temple, it was obvious everyone else was in the same condition I was, though nobody else had been cut off for damn near a week. My hands were shaking so badly Jim poured my wine for me, which the rest of the guys thought was hilarious. I didn't give a shit.

I couldn't keep my eyes off the open bathroom door. The lights were low in there now. Candlelight flickered on the reflective tile, and the girls were splashing. I slowly drained my glass, ignoring the conversation around me as the sounds in the bathroom quietened to low murmurs. My cock throbbed as I imagined what they were doing in there. Four women naked in a huge tub, three of them pleasuring the fourth as a goddess. Four sets of naked breasts, four pussies – Merlina's shaved satiny smooth, maybe the others as well – four beautiful female behinds. I caught my hand as it was sneaking towards my dick.

'You may come in,' Kay called.

We didn't even pretend to walk slowly but hurried to the bathroom.

The scene was even hotter than I'd imagined. Merlina was stretched out naked on the steaming water, her well-oiled body floating in her friends' arms. Her eyes were closed. Her head rested on a large, contoured bath pillow, her hair caught up in a tortoiseshell clip that held her tiara perfectly in place. Audrey knelt under one arm, her back to us, her short black hair framing her pert young face. Her arms supported Merlina's torso from that side. Her wide-open lips covered Merlina's entire nipple. Audrey was sucking hard and rhythmically, drawing Merlina's breast deep into her mouth. The low groans from Merlina's barely parted lips told me how much she was enjoying Audrey's ministrations.

Elaine knelt on the other side, her short blonde curls damp with sweat. Her large full breasts floated on the surface of the water. Her voluptuous curves were pressed close to Merlina's other side, one arm underneath and supporting. The other hand was fingering Merlina's stiff, glistening nipple–pulling and tugging and rolling it the way my oh-so-libidinous wife loved. Elaine was kissing her way up Merlina's neck, the short sweet nips interspersed with long, wet, deep tongue probes between Merlina's lips. I've never been able to kiss the way women do–slow and patient and tasting. I get too carried away. No matter how hard I try to slow down, when I get really turned on, Merlina says I go too fast and get too rough, especially if I haven't shaved. I'd shaved three times today. Elaine was kissing my wife the way a goddess should be kissed.

Kay sat neck-deep in the water between my wife's legs, her long dark curls also caught up in a jewelled clip on top of her head. Merlina's thighs rested on Kay's shoulders, Merlina's creamy shaved labia spread so wide I could see Kay's tongue licking deep into the dark-pink folds. Eating pussy is something I'm good at. I can make Merlina come every time. Still, there was something gentler in the way Kay was doing it. Something more tender and feminine and mysterious that was turning Merlina on very slowly. I had the feeling that secret womanly something was going to make Merlina come even harder than I could.

Kay slid her arms under Merlina's hips. She leaned closer, her hands curling up and around Merlina's waist, then down to spread Merlina's labia further. Merlina's stiff pink clit poked up right in front of Kay's mouth. Kay's tongue flicked out again, directly onto the centre of that glistening bundle of nerves. Merlina bucked and cried out, thrusting her hips up to meet Kay's ruthlessly flailing tongue. Kay smiled, and kept her tongue moving.

'You ordered us to awaken your body, goddess,' Elaine said quietly. 'Are we doing it correctly?'

If they'd been doing it any more correctly, Merlina would have been screaming.

'More,' she panted. 'Harder. Fingers, too. My servants by the door, remove your slave belts and put your hands on your dicks. You may worship me from afar.'

I threw the pre-come-soaked G-string aside and shuddered as my hand closed around my shaft. Masturbating in front of anyone, even Merlina, embarrassed me so much. I rarely did it even at birthday celebrations. Doing it now in front of all my closest friends, when I was so desperately, uncontrollably horny, was almost more than I could stand. I stroked slowly up, trembling as I kept my eyes glued to the sight of my glorious goddess wife being serviced by her attendants.

Kay lifted one hand, wiggling her two middle fingers. Elaine fumbled at the side of the tub and caught the bottle of silicone oil resting on the edge. She poured a thick, steady stream over Kay's fingers. Then she set the bottle down and kissed her way over Merlina's neck. Elaine's tongue trailed around the soft weight of Merlina's breast, teasing the nipple until it stood up long and hard. Then Elaine opened her mouth wide, and sucked in Merlina's entire areola.

Merlina gasped. But, instead of relaxing into the sensation the way she usually did, she jumped again. Her breath came out in a long, shaky sigh, and she lay there trembling.

I frowned. Kay was using only one hand to hold Merlina's labia open. The other hand, the one Elaine had drenched in lube, was moving beneath the water. Her middle fingers were hidden, her thumb wiggling just below her still-flailing tongue. Normally, Merlina moaned and relaxed when I put my fingers in her pussy. Then Kay's thumb slid under the water, too. Merlina moaned all right, but the trembling increased.

Oh, fuck. If Kay's thumb was in Merlina's pussy, that meant Kay's other fingers were … up Merlina's ass.

I didn't do that often. Merlina said she wanted me to, but my fingers were too rough. Kay's fingers were smaller than mine, and she had at least two, maybe three of them up my wife's ass. Obviously, I had some major learning to do in that department. Kay's arm was moving in long, firm strokes, rocking Merlina's body with each thrust. When she sucked Merlina's clit into her mouth,

Kay's cheeks moved in tandem with her arm, harder, stronger. Elaine's and Audrey's sucking was picking up the rhythm, too. Stronger, but still so incredibly gentle.

'Don't stop,' Merlina panted. 'Make me come. I want to come. *Come!*' The last word was an order, and it ended on a squeal. Merlina bucked up, screaming and flailing as water splashed over the side of the tub. Elaine and Audrey and Kay held her tight, sucking and pumping and keeping Merlina's head above water as she screamed and came again. Finally, Merlina choked out, 'Enough!' and relaxed into the arms of her happy, laughing girlfriends.

I came in my hand. From the sounds around me, I wasn't the only one. I didn't care who was looking at me. Now I knew why Merlina had insisted on 'anticipation'. She wanted to make sure I'd be up for more than one round of worshipping her by masturbation in her goddess fantasy. Oh, baby, I was up for it!

We men waited patiently at the side of the room, surreptitiously wiping ourselves with hand towels while the girls re-enacted Botticelli's *Birth of Venus* painting. Kay and Elaine and Audrey led Merlina from the tub, then dried her and each other with soft fluffy towels. They hooked Merlina's garter belt around her waist, eased the white silk stockings back up her long, elegant legs and pulled the lacy thong up over her glistening bare labia. Then they strapped on her heels and pulled the slinky white dress down over her glistening, well-pampered curves.

As Audrey blew out the candles, Elaine picked up a handful of green velvet ribbons and tied each man's cock in a below-the-balls-and-over-the-shaft cock ring that left no doubt we'd all be ready to serve our goddess. Then Kay picked up a bowl of pink silk rose petals and, throwing the petals on the floor in front of her, led her still naked, giggling sisters into the main room.

Someone – I assumed it was Jim – had dimmed the lights to a soft golden glow. Moments later, Merlina was settled on a long, low couch, Elaine feeding her grapes and tidbits of cheese and Audrey holding a goblet of wine to her lips. Kay threw a pillow on the floor, knelt beside her and quietly slid a hand inside the top of Merlina's dress. Merlina purred and tipped her head back, taking a deep swallow of wine. She licked her lips and pointed a finger at me.

'You. Massage my feet. You –' she pointed at Audrey's husband, Mike '– eat my pussy. I want a lot of tongue on my clit.'

I wanted to eat her pussy! But Mike was on his knees in a heartbeat. He leaned over the bottom of the couch, lifted Merlina's dress just enough to slide his face under it and put her legs on his shoulders. Then he pulled the thong to one side and went to town. As Merlina moaned, I caught a foot and eased the gorgeous strappy sandal from her toes. Then I dug my fingers deep into the silk-covered arch of her delicate, shapely foot, just the way she liked it. Her moans got even louder.

'Nobody else gets to come,' she panted. 'Not until I'm satisfied.'

With that single command, the rest of us set to serving her with renewed determination.

Merlina was insatiable. One minute she had the front of her dress pulled open with Audrey and Stan sucking her nipples and me fucking her cunt. The only thing that kept me from shooting despite her command was the condom that was *de rigueur* for our group sex. Then Merlina straddled Kay's face, her clit pressing down on Kay's constantly moving lips, while Jim knelt in back of them, his face in Merlina's crack, tonguing deep up her behind. She sucked Elaine's huge, heavy breasts almost to bruises, sucking all the way through both their loud, wailing climaxes while I finger-fucked both their pussies. Then she sucked every well-trussed set of cock and balls in the room until we pleaded with her to let us come. She didn't. Not even when she wailed through two more orgasms.

She finally had mercy on Jim and Mike and Stan, ordering each wife, one at a time, to work a well-lubed finger up her husband's ass and suck him to climax while the others watched. Then she ordered the husbands to reciprocate, though she gave Stan permission to bury his face in Elaine's crack before he finger-fucked her to her own screaming orgasm.

At Merlina's direction, I sucked her nipples while she

watched. The ecstatic reactions throughout the room told me we were going to be seeing variations on this theme at many other birthdays in the future. Then Merlina told me it was my turn. She pulled her dress off and threw it on the floor. Then she lay down on one of the queen-sized beds in just her garter belt and stockings.

I swallowed hard and obediently followed her orders to get in a 69 position over her. I buried my face in her pussy, groaning as she swallowed my cock. Then her finger brushed at my backdoor. I stiffened, my face heating with the most embarrassment, the most vulnerability and submission I'd ever felt in my life.

Merlina rubbed, letting me kiss her silky smooth pussy lips, but only the lips, until the tension flowed from my body. Cool lube slicked over me again. I shivered as her slick finger slid slowly in.

'Don't come,' Merlina said softly, her lips kissing slowly up the side of my shaft. 'Put your finger in me, just like I'm putting mine in you.'

Her glistening pucker winked softly in front of me. I held my hand out. Someone, I think it was Kay, squeezed lubricant on my finger. Then I was rubbing Merlina's sphincter, brushing the edges, then slowly sliding my finger in and out, mimicking every move she was doing to me.

'That's it,' she said quietly. 'I think you've got it now.' She took a deep, shaking breath. 'Roll over on your back.'

I did, my backdoor still quivering as Merlina rose up and knelt over me, facing my feet. I'd long since lost the condom. A feminine hand rolled a new one on me. I couldn't see who. All three of the women were kneeling by the couch on the other side of Merlina. Then Merlina slowly lowered her pussy onto my cock, fucking me until I was fighting not to come in spite of the cock ring. She leaned forwards, my shaft buried to the hilt, and took a deep breath.

'Put your finger up my bottom, but do it slowly and gently, just the way I showed you. We're not going to have any more of your ham-fisted roughness. I want slow, tender pumping that makes me come really hard. Believe me, honey, I'll make it worth your while.'

This time, I did it right. I slid my finger up her silky soft bottom–just as a slick female finger slid up my back door. A gentle hand cupped my balls and started to tug. Then Merlina untied the velvet ribbon around my cock. Matching the finger inside me touch for touch, I finger-fucked my goddess's bottom, just the way she liked it, just the way she deserved, while she milked my cock with her ultra-talented pussy until, this time, we cried out together.

I must have dozed off, because the next thing I knew, the guys were hauling me up to sing 'Happy Birthday'. We lounged on the mattresses, clearing a path through the incredibly delicious food as we took turns feeding

Merlina and talked about how this was the best birthday fantasy ever and how we should do it again next year – if it pleased our goddess to do so, of course. The look in Merlina's eyes told me it wasn't going to be anywhere near that long before she had her finger up my bottom again – and I had mine up hers, this time doing it right.

'Happy birthday, goddess,' I said with a grin, toasting her with another glass of wine.

Merlina giggled and I stuffed another grape in her mouth.

'The day's not over for another twenty minutes.' She pushed me on the couch and straddled my now thoroughly exhausted cock. I raised my eyebrow as she lifted a well-sucked nipple to my lips.

'I'm too tired to fuck anymore,' she said, smiling. 'But a bit more nipple-sucking would end the day really well for me.'

Far be it from me to deny my goddess on her birthday. I opened my mouth, took her breast in both hands and we indulged.

Live to Serve
Kathleen Tudor

Luis weighed the order ticket in his hand a moment, but he knew he was really weighing his options. The order was perfect – a Reuben that would take only a few minutes to cook and a steak sandwich, well done. His professional pride pricked him for a moment, but then his hand drifted down to his side and, as if acting on its own, touched the place in his pocket where the crisp $50 bill was folded away.

He sighed as he made the decision he'd already known he was going to make. He felt bad for Rose – she seemed like a nice girl – but his family could make an extra $50 here and there stretch pretty far. He wasn't sure if the bossman wanted her gone or just liked to give her grief, but she was going to have to deal with it on her own.

He tossed the corned beef onto the grill alongside the sauerkraut, and then transferred them to a pair of rye slices slathered with Thousand Island. He only put the thick New York strip onto the grill when the sandwich was already assembled and grilling. That poor girl was just going to have to take care of herself.

***

Rose had known what was coming all day, ever since a late lunch order had been botched, with one sandwich coming out nearly ten minutes before the other. Her eyes flew frequently to her little gold watch as she wondered how much longer it would be before he called for her; it was a struggle to maintain the normal, polite façade that garnered her a decent amount of money every evening in tips.

She was carrying a stack of dirty dishes in one arm and mentally reciting an order she'd just taken when she heard the three words that always knocked her out of her regularly scheduled orbit. 'Freddy wants you.'

'Thanks,' she said, sounding faint and squeaky even to her own ears. She dropped off the dirty dishes and went to the computer to enter the order as quickly as she could, having to consult her notes since the anticipation had pushed the details out of her head. It only took a couple of minutes, but a second co-worker had already been dispatched to find her by the time she was done.

'Freddy said you're to come to the office, now,' said

Katie, looking nervous. 'I'm supposed to take your tables while you're busy. Anything I need to know?'

'Twelve needs to order. Other than that, just keep an eye on the window and drinks,' Rose replied, trying to keep her voice steady. Her nerves were jangling and she felt her muscles quiver. 'Thanks, Katie.'

Katie shrugged, probably preferring not to get too closely acquainted with the woman the boss had targeted, and brushed past Rose on her way to the salad-prep station. Rose took a breath, brushed her hands down her apron. Nothing left to do, she went around the corner and through the door that would take her into the inner area of the kitchen and, through that, to the office.

The office door was thick to block out kitchen noise, but at the moment it was propped open and waiting for her. She paused, wishing she'd had time to check her hair and makeup, then brushed the thought away and stepped through the doorway.

Freddy was inside, seated in the swivel chair that looked like it belonged in an executive suite instead of a crowded, messy restaurant office. 'Shut the door.'

Rose did so, waiting until it had closed all the way before she turned to face Freddy, lowered her head and clasped her hands before her. 'Yes, Master.'

'Do you know why you're here?' he asked in a quiet, serious tone.

'I have an idea, Master.' She kept the irony out of her

voice, barely, since she was fairly sure he'd somehow arranged her earlier problems.

'You've gotten another complaint, Rose. I'm told that you brought cold food out to a customer at lunchtime today.'

Rose had long since learned not to protest her innocence or mention that it wasn't her fault what happened in the kitchens. A shiver went through her, and she kept her eyes on Freddy's black boots. 'Yes, Master.'

'It seems to me that this kind of behaviour must be punished. Don't you think so, girl?' He shifted in his seat and she allowed her eyes to flick up high enough to see that his erection strained against his zipper as if it was perfectly aware what came next. She took a deep breath through her nose as she forced her eyes back to the heavy boots.

'Yes, Master, the girl deserves to be punished,' she said in a voice that barely came out above a whisper.

'Take your hair down.'

'Yes, Master,' Rose said, her hands already moving to free her long, wavy blonde hair from the bun that kept it contained while she worked. As she pulled the elastic free, her hair tumbled down around her shoulders and she shook it out for him, knowing how he loved to watch the shimmering waves in motion. He made a small sound of arousal and approval and she felt the tingles that had already started in her cunt intensify at the noise.

166

'Take it out,' he said, his own voice husky. His hands still rested on the armrests of his huge chair as he waited.

'Yes, Master,' she whispered again. She knelt on the concrete floor between his legs to put herself close to his straining cock and slowly, carefully worked the button and zipper of his trousers to allow it to spring free. The musky scent of him overtook her and she nearly swooned at the headiness of it.

Freddy made a low sound in his throat as she freed him. 'Now let's see how sorry you are. Open,' he said. Rose opened her mouth wide and waited patiently. He stared at her for a long moment, forcing her to hold the embarrassing position before he finally grabbed the hair at the back of her head and guided her down onto his cock. 'Oh, yes. That's good.'

Rose closed her eyes and focused on keeping her throat open the way that he had taught her. Master slowly pushed her head down onto his cock, forcing the hard length of it past her tongue and down her throat. She took breaths through her nose when she could, though it was all she could do not to pant in desire as he oh-so-slowly fucked her throat.

'That's right, this is all you're good for, isn't it? Isn't it?' He held his cock deep in her throat, grinding back and forth to fully enjoy the sensation until she made a noise that even she wasn't sure was gagging or agreement. Maybe it was both. He pulled out all the way and then thrust hard into her throat, forcing her to gag again, and she felt her pussy grow even heavier and wetter as he used her.

She couldn't see his face, but she knew that it would be flushed with the power and the pleasure of having her at his feet and in his control. His moans filled the small space, but even his utterances were short, tight, controlled, just like his slow movements of her head up and down on his erection. Rose whimpered as he shifted his tight grip in her hair, and Freddy made a satisfied sound.

'That's right, you take your punishment. You take whatever I give you.'

She could have laughed at that, since this was truly her gift to him. It had been her idea from the very beginning, this arrangement of theirs. She wouldn't dare laugh, though. Not when he was in control like this.

She'd first met Freddy at a BDSM club, where they'd played a handful of times in some rough and pleasurable scenes. She'd enjoyed his intensity and the way that he pushed her to her limits where other men had been too afraid to take her. Not that he was cruel – he was careful, always – but he also knew exactly how much punishment she could take, and she gloried in taking it.

'That's right, you whore, you're lucky I don't just kick your ass to the kerb and let you make your way on a corner where you belong.'

He wouldn't, of course – didn't even file the complaints he caused for her – but the words made her moan with arousal anyway. Her nipples were rough and hard against her shirt. He groaned in reaction to the vibrations of her throat against his cock, and slid deep into her throat.

They'd both been equally shocked a year ago when she had shown up in his office for the interview and they had seen one another. She could remember thinking that it was probably the first time he had seen her clothed and, based on his shocked expression, he was only thinking of the fastest way to get rid of her. But when he'd pulled Rose aside for her 'interview' and whispered urgently that he thought it would be best if she just left, quickly, she put on her sexiest smile and made him a different proposition. 'There's no reason work and play can't overlap a bit as long as we're discreet,' she'd said, and she'd let her smile turn sweet as she dipped her head in submissive posture to seal the deal with a 'Sir'.

He had inhaled then, as sharply and quickly as he did now when she swallowed around his cock, caressing him with the depths of her throat, and her lips curved just a little as she recalled his answer. 'No. Master.'

And familiarity had bred something so much more astonishingthan even the most incredible play sessions they had ever had. Just looking at him at work some days could make her pussy hot and wet, and she would move through her day in a haze of lust, wondering if this would be one of those special days.

A day like today. Rose moaned again as she thought of how lucky she was to be kneeling between this man's legs with her lips wrapped around his cock, and then again at the sweet humiliation of knowing that, outside this office, everyone was whispering about the dressing down that they assumed she was getting. If only they knew the truth …

'Open your shirt,' Master said, and she hurried to comply, nearly fumbling the buttons in her haste to obey. Rose had learned to wear front-clasp bras to work in anticipation of his desires – things went more smoothly if she could give him maximum access with a minimum of undressing or fussing.

When the shirt was open he reached down with his free hand – still slowly and carefully lowering her onto his cock with his other fist in her hair – and popped the clasp on her bra. She whimpered around his cock and delighted in his moaned reply. He ran the back of his fingers from the centre of her chest across the surface of one breast, pushing the bra out of the way as he went.

The gentle touch contrasted so strongly with the rough way he handled her hair that her clit tingled as if it was about to explode, but she knew better than to seek release without his permission. Instead, she waited, purring her delight when his fingers turned, found her nipple and latched on, squeezing hard and twisting to shoot an exquisite pain through her breast. He maintained that grip, squeezing so hard she was sure to bruise around her nipple, as he increased the pace of his pleasure.

His hand on the back of her head forced her down fast and immediately tore her up again, and suddenly she was whimpering and moaning and crying out in earnest as he forced himself deep into her throat over and over in delicious, painful pleasure. Rose struggled and failed to hold her throat open and receptive to the invasion, and his arousal at the sounds of her choking and gagging was unmistakable.

'Swallow it all. Oh, *fuck*.' And then he drove deep into her and held himself there, his pulsing cock emptying down her throat.

He pulled away when he was finished, leaving a trail of come across her face as he slid free of her, and she gasped to regain her breath.

'Thank you, Master,' Rose said as soon as she was capable of speech again.

His smile was pleased as he reached down to place a vice-like grip on her other nipple. 'You look like a real whore, you know,' he told her in a neutral tone.

Her answer was a gasp as he tightened and twisted with both hands at once, pulling upwards to draw her to her feet by the nipples. She moaned in helpless pain and pleasure as she followed his lead until she was standing

171

before him, her hair a mess, makeup running from the tears that had streamed from her eyes as she gagged, and her shirt open, breasts exposed to his ruthless touch. 'I want to bend you over and stick my cock in you right now.'

They didn't have time, but the image was sufficient to cause another whimper of arousal. He sighed and stood in front of her, grabbed her hair and bent her head back. She stared at the ceiling, back bowed, and felt him lift one heavy breast and bite down hard, marking her. He laughed at her desperate moans, knowing she'd be soaked through her panties and would have to finish her shift that way. 'Clean yourself up,' he said, releasing her. 'What time do you get off?'

'Five,' she said, though he knew already since he was in charge of the schedules.

'Good. And do you have plans tonight?'

'No, Master.' This was unusual, and she felt a thrill through her body.

'Then have dinner on the table at six. You have my key?'

'Yes, Master.' He'd given it to her very recently, in fact, and she had been honoured enough to want to carry it with her all the time.

He nodded to her as she finished buttoning her shirt. She reached up to brush her hair back up and twist it into a bun, and he smiled and brushed his semen off her cheek.

'I love the look of you with your hands together behind your head like that,' he teased, and she blushed and lowered her head as much as she could without messing up her style-in-progress. His comments during play were hot and exciting, but it was gentle moments like this that had pushed their relationship out of the bedroom. And office.

Freddy gave her one last proprietary kiss before approving her appearance. Rose smiled, then put on a properly chastised face and fled the office as if she was barely in control of herself. She would clean up her makeup in the bathroom before returning to her shift – her tearstained face would only confirm for everyone else that she had been reprimanded in the traditional manner.

She couldn't help humming softly as she wiped her face clean and reapplied her lipstick, however. She was already considering her plans for his dinner.

* * *

Rose kept her head down and drifted through the rest of her shift, and the other staff kept their distance from her as if her bad luck were contagious. She made sure to be done with all of her work by five on the dot, even letting Katie take a few of her tables towards the end of her shift so that she wouldn't risk being late.

Freddy lived only ten minutes away, but her own apartment was farther and in the wrong direction, so she wouldn't be able to change her clothes. If she hurried, though, she might have time to shower before cooking dinner.

When she got to his house, she found that he'd made it easy. His fridge was stocked with asparagus and a steak thawing on a plate, and she tossed a few red potatoes in a pot to boil for mashing before she hurried to the bathroom to shower. She put on his robe to walk her clothes to the car, knowing he wouldn't want her work clothing in his house, but she returned the robe when she got back inside.

It was a close thing, but the asparagus was roasted, the dry-rubbed steak grilled and the potatoes mashed and all of it plated just moments before she heard his key turn in the door. She grinned as she lifted the plate and stepped into the heels she'd brought in from her car. She was naked except for the heels – which she'd started to carry in her trunk for just such occasions – and she straightened her spine and allowed herself to sway on them to best show off her assets as she met him in the dining room.

Master gave her an appreciative look as she set the plate down beside his waiting water glass just as he sat. 'Exquisite timing, my pet,' he said, and waved her off.

She smiled, and a thrill went through her at knowing

she had passed some sort of test. She moved to stand behind his right shoulder to wait. After his second bite, he speared a small piece of the steak and held it up over his shoulder. She leaned forwards and daintily ate it.

He ate in silence at first, pensive, and she kept her place and ate each second or third bite, which he offered to her in the same way. 'I had to punish a girl today,' he said suddenly, and she started at the sound of his voice in the quiet room. He took a mouthful of the potatoes and then held an asparagus tip up for her to nibble. 'She was a very lazy girl, not like you, my dear.' She could hear the smile in his voice, and it made her wet to hear about her own punishment like this.

Master took a slow sip of the water and continued. 'She brought cold food to one of our customers. I couldn't tolerate that, could I?'

He paused, so she answered, 'No, Master.'

'No, of course I couldn't. I had to teach her a lesson. I brought her to my office and told her I should fire her, and she begged me to keep her job. Said she had mouths to feed and she was too stupid to do anything else, but she promised she would do *anything* if I wouldn't fire her.' He took another bite and Rose felt her breath and pulse quicken as she waited to hear how he would tell the story.

'I told her that she would have to show me how important her job was to her, so she dropped to her knees, and begged me to let her suck me off, right there in the office.' His voice was even, but she had learned to hear the pleasure behind his words. She shuddered in arousal as he carelessly lifted another piece of steak and she leaned forwards to daintily take it from the fork.

He'd bound her once, knotting a crotch rope so that it rubbed against her clit every time she bent forwards to take a morsel from him. She'd been whimpering with arousal by the time he'd finished his meal; he was sharing much more with her than normal, just to hear her pant. He'd barely finished the last bite before he'd thrown her on the table and fucked her hard, rope and all. She was nearly as aroused by the memory as she was by the story he was spinning as he fed her.

'Well, I couldn't deny her the chance to prove herself, could I, my dear?'

'No, Master.'

'That's right, it would have been cruel of me! So I let that little slut put my cock in her mouth, and then I grabbed her by the hair and fucked her throat like she deserved. It felt so good, pounding deep into her throat like that.'

He paused, so she dared to interject, 'You were very kind, Master.'

He chuckled at that, and she smiled. She remembered the feel of his cock sliding into her throat, the head pushing past the base of her tongue again and again as she gave him pleasure. He'd taken her and used her, and there were few things that could get her wetter than that. Her thighs were growing sticky with arousal and Master must have noticed, because he took a deep breath, made a pleased sound and fed her the last bite of his steak.

'I'm ready for my dessert,' he said.

She froze, panicked. He hadn't asked for dessert, and Rose hadn't had time to prepare anything but the meal.

'There is a bowl of strawberries in the fridge. Bring it.'

She let out her breath and hurried to retrieve the cold bowl of berries. Master had pushed his dishes to the far side of the table by the time she returned.

'I'll be having strawberries and cream,' he said.

She paused, confused, since he hadn't told her to look for cream, but he gestured to the table and suddenly she understood.

'Oh your knees, if you will.'

'Yes, Master,' she said, and climbed up onto the table. She turned her back to him, kneeling with her legs spread so that her cunt was exposed for him. It was a shock when the first icy cold berry was pressed against her dripping hole. He swirled it there, and she whimpered as the heat of her body and the cold of the fruit contrasted. She heard him bite into it and pictured that juicy red flesh flavoured with her cream, and whimpered again.

One of his hands stroked up her leg on the inside, petting and caressing, and this time she jumped slightly when the startling cold was pressed against hercunt. 'Mmm, delicious,' he said, and she moaned, wanting so much more than a cold berry against her lips. Rose wanted to be filled, to be fucked, to be used hard and brought to pleasure. The teasing was a beautiful torture.

Master moved his hand from her leg to her cunt and thrust two fingers inside. She clenched around him, wanting to push back against him and encourage him to fuck her. Instead, she held herself still, panting loudly with arousal. Master chuckled as he slowly finger-fucked her before withdrawing his hand from her body. Another cold berry pressed against her folds and he swirled it through her cream, drawing it up to rub it against her clit, then bringing it to his mouth and sucking it loudly before biting into it.

'Do you want to come?' he asked.

'Please, Master! Yes, Master!'

She heard his chair scrape back as he stood up behind her, and suddenly his fingers returned to her cunt, plunging into her and fucking her roughly. 'Do you enjoy your job?'

The question was so out of place that for a moment her lust-addled mind couldn't wrap around it. 'Yes, Master,' she finally said, trying to focus on his query despite the distraction of his fingers thrusting roughly into her body.

'I mean it. Would you choose to work there if you didn't have to?'

'I don't – I mean – I don't know, Master. It's just a job, but it's not a bad one.' Rose was proud of how she'd managed to answer without screaming, although her voice was breathy with arousal and she'd ended the sentence with a moan.

His hands suddenly withdrew from her and she cried out at the sudden lack of sensation after the overwhelming pleasure.

'Because it seems to me that, if you'd like to quit, no one would be surprised after how you looked coming out of my office today.' His voice was calm, suggestive, and when he finished speaking she heard a clatter and saw a slim silver chain with a dainty padlock slide to a rest between her hands. He'd tossed the collar onto the table for her to see.

'But my apartment –' A collar. Had he just offered her a collar?

'If you move in,' he said, 'you wouldn't have to worry about working. Well, not for money, anyway.'

Rose knelt on a table in the middle of her boss's dining room, naked, her cunt exposed for him and a chain collar resting between her hands as her juices slicked his fingers. It vied for the most erotic, most ridiculous and most romantic moment of her life, and she couldn't help but laugh.

'Are you asking me?' she enquired, breathless. It somehow felt wrong to turn and look at him in this moment, so she kept her eyes lowered, staring at the beautiful symbol on the table before her.

'I'd miss the midday rendezvous, but ... housekeeper, cook, sex slave ... sound like the kind of life you want, my Rose?'

'Will you put it on me?'

'Is that a yes?'

'Yes.'

'Yes, what?' he said, his voice moving from the softness of his invitation to the tone of command she'd always known.

'Yes, Master,' she said.

He grabbed her hips and thrust his cock into her then. Rose hadn't heard his zipper, but he must have pulled himself out in anticipation of exactly this moment.

'Then come for me.'

As he drove himself deep inside her, she clenched around him and finally felt herself release. She screamed as she came, pleasure shooting through her as he rode her hard. She was just coming down from the first exquisite orgasm when he reached up to tangle one fist in her hair. He wrenched her head back hard and used it to pull her back onto his cock, thrusting into her as if he meant to spear her. He reached around with his other hand to find her clit and pinched it, hard, and her body seemed to dissolve as the pleasure and pain mingled in a second, blinding orgasm.

She was only vaguely aware of his own triumphant roar of pleasure as he continued to pound into her. As she came back to herself, she realised that she was lying on her side on the table, her eyes closed, her breath coming in hard, heavy gasps. She heard a click at her throat and opened her eyes to see Freddy holding the closed lock, the chain now tight–though not uncomfortably so–around her throat.

'You are *mine*,' he said, and his eyes were fierce and gentle all at the same time.

Rose smiled, putting her love for the man into her voice as she agreed. 'Yes, Master.'